STALKING SECOND

STALKING SECOND

AN ALL ABOUT THE DIAMOND ROMANCE

NAOMI SPRINGTHORP

Stalking Second
An All About the Diamond Romance (Book 7)
Copyright © 2024 Naomi Springthorp
Published by Naomi Springthorp
All rights reserved
Print Edition ISBN 978-1-949243-52-9

An All About the Diamond Romance series is a work of fiction and does not in any way advocate irresponsible behavior. This book contains content that is not suitable for readers 17 and under. Please store your files where they cannot be accessed by minors.

Cover Photographer: Tonya Clark Photography - All About the Covers
Cover Model: Sean Brady
Graphic Designer: Irene Johnson johnsoni@mac.com
Editor: Katrina Fair

For everyone who's allowed love to guide you.

CHAPTER ONE

Maggie

W hy is he here? I can't see his face, but I'd recognize him anywhere with his built muscular shoulders, solid slender core, perfect butt, and miles of legs. The university's annual Researching the Sciences banquet is the last place I'd ever expect to find him. It's a pleasant surprise, and makes attending this event worth my time. Historically, I've attended everything he does, and that's just it. I can't say this is a first, it doesn't truly count, because I didn't invite him or tell him I was being honored tonight—he's just here. He was at one of my tennis tournaments back in my freshman year, but I'm pretty sure that was simply coincidence. This is silly, why would I invite him? It's not like he's my boyfriend, maybe not even a friend. I just happen to have an, um, let's call it an appreciation for his *work* both on the field and in the workout room.

Then again, what if he... There's no way. If he had any idea he was being watched while he was in the shower, he'd have pulled the curtain and probably called the police. And if he had caught me, I'd have lost my job by now. Huh, maybe I should have thought about that ahead of time. My job provides a dominant part of the research for my thesis. I didn't calculate this into the risk I've been taking. I should stop. I don't want to lose my job, nor be arrested. Though, this could be a case of those things that make smart girls stupid—and in case you need to ask, his adonis belt is hard cut. None of this was my intent. Things just... happened.

He won't recognize me tonight in my navy-blue cocktail dress, with my long dark hair down in fluffy curls instead of up in a tight ponytail in my denim shorts and T-shirt or over-sized hoodie. That's what I've worn to his games since junior high when I became scorekeeper. I've been his baseball team's scorekeeper every year through high school and college. Now that I'm in the master's program, I've landed the Statistician job for the San Diego Seals and attend every home game to keep score for myself—statistics mean nothing if the numbers aren't gathered accurately in the first place, so I take it on myself to keep score and compare with the score-keeper. It's the perfect job for working on my thesis on the comparison of projected statistics compared to actual outcome, and the value they provide to a sports administration. I've attended every one of his home baseball games for eleven seasons, not to mention three years of high school basketball. I've lived through my dad's fanatical infatuation with the San Diego Seals since I was born and listened to him and his buddies discuss the game for hours on end. Basically, my thesis is Skill, Chemistry, or Moneyball? And I believe there is actually a ratio of these three things that need to be combined to have a successful winning team.

No, I'm not concerned. I blend into the woodwork, and dressed like this? There's no chance he recognizes me.

CHAPTER TWO

Drew

Walking up to the university auditorium I remind myself why I'm here and why I spent the money on this tuxedo. I've lived and played sports in San Diego all of my life, except for the couple of years I spent in the minors, and I want to keep it that way. I made a conscious decision to be more active and supportive in my community, so this season when the San Diego Seals' marketing team came around with requests for players to attend community functions and be the face of the team, I volunteered for as many as I could. Many of my teammates thanked me for biting the bullet for them, but I don't see it that way. This is my home. This will always be my home. I want to support the local people who are trying to make our world a better place. So, here I am at my first event, the Researching the Sciences banquet, hoping my minor in Physics might help me through conversations this evening.

I expected to find a quiet room filled with mostly men in

suits. The marketing department assured me that I should wear a tux, that's appropriate for a cocktail banquet. Still, I imagined older men in corduroy coats with suede patches at the elbows and a fruit punch bowl with orange slices floating in it. Yet, I wore my tux anyway because I don't want to chance being under dressed when I'm representing the team, though I'm sure that some of my teammates would've worn their jersey. I'd bet at least one of them has a custom tuxedo with their name and number on the back of it. I went for the clean 007 look. Stepping into the auditorium I'm surprised by the boisterous crowd and trays full of champagne flutes circulating the room.

Suddenly the room falls silent. The crowd of people parts like Moses parting the sea and becomes nothing but an indiscernible blur with a spotlight shining bright on a gorgeous and for some reason familiar woman. I keep my distance and revere her beauty as I try to figure out why she's so familiar to me. Her dark blue cocktail dress accentuates everything about her. Its wide ties are knotted behind her neck and hang elegantly down her back, almost hiding that the dress is backless. Hugging her curves from her waist to just above her knees with a layer of relaxed chiffon hanging over it and longer in the back. Metallic silver high-heeled shoes with a peek-a-boo toe that match the light beading on the upper bodice. Long brunette hair that's got curl and a feminine softness to it topping off her look. She finally turns around and her eyes sparkle nearly as much as her smile. The light shines from behind her outlining her slender figure through the chiffon skirt. I focus on her face, her makeup applied light and clean with a shiny lip gloss. I can't place her as I continue to observe.

CHAPTER THREE

Maggie

Three weeks earlier...

There's something serene and surreal about watching the game from the press box. Well, that's basically where I sit. The view is phenomenal, offering every square inch of the field. The official Scorekeeper has his own space with a desk next to the press box and I sit in the chair closest to him so I can ask him questions and we can compare notes. I should have the title Assistant Scorekeeper for how many times he's referred to me or I've caught him with incorrect or incomplete scorekeeping. Reason number one for why I keep score: I don't trust his scorekeeping, and statistics are only as good as the numbers they're derived from.

The team has settled into a steady lineup with Seno catching, Martin on first base, Brandt on second base, Prince on third base, Mason at shortstop, Lucine in left field, Cross in center field, and Rock in right field. It makes it easier when they're all where they belong and not shuffled around with off days or trying to fill a spot for a player on the injured list. I track statistics for the team as a whole and each of the individual players. I track the statistics for the opposing team while they're visiting as well, but that's mostly for my own entertainment and research. I like to compare how the Seals are doing. But sometimes there's an obvious anomaly and the coach is always happy to get that information. For example, some batters never swing at the first pitch and others always swing at the first pitch, but it can change throughout the season. Coaches like confirmation.

The Seals have been playing well. The last couple of seasons they've come up just shy of making it to the post-season. This year may be different. They've been playing tight and their collective stats have been getting better over-all. (I actually charted it to get a visual of their progress.) Tonight's game is a textbook example of their progress. They move together like a precision machine. Plays are made to look as simple as 1-2-3 and the baseballs pop off their bats. Cross has been progressing faster than the others, while Seno is the player they all want to play like. Rock and Lucine are doing their best and maintaining, but my guess is they're both near retirement. Mason is pushing to keep up with Cross, and achieves it in his hitting, but not on the bases. Martin and Brandt have a silent communication on the field, don't get in their crosshairs or you'll be out—both above average. Drew Brandt is quiet and efficient on the field, not flashy.

The game ended at 5-2 Seals with Brandt smashing a two-run homer for a couple of insurance runs in the seventh inning, and the team playing some small ball to bring one after the other around to score in the third inning.

Drew crouches like a frog at second to keep loose. He has long muscular legs so it's kind of funny to see but also sexy as hell. His stats say he's 6'4" and 190 pounds. He's always been tall. His copper-colored hair has an unruly wave to it and he keeps it cut fairly short but sometimes allows the ends to start to curl at his neck. His eyes are a gorgeous clear blue outlined with fiery black flecks. He always smells intoxicating and there's something about his shoulders, the way he holds himself, that drives me crazy. So what, maybe I've had a crush on him since junior high. He's perfect.

I stop everything to observe as he walks off the field. Masculine. Broad shoulders that move in time with the rest of his body, exemplifying his coordination and strength. All I want to do is get his shirt off of him and explore his professionally honed body.

I REVIEW the stats for the game. I've been watching the difference in play over the innings and progression of the game and noting who the pitcher is. The closer, Houck, doesn't really impact this because he's next to perfect, but the relief pitchers are another story and are proving to be less consistent. Proof of why he's the closer, but someday that will change and my stats will be the first place it's discovered.

I double check all of my numbers, save a copy for my research, and submit them to the Seals along with my notes on the game.

I gather my notebook, laptop, and collection of pens and colored pencils, getting it all packed away in my backpack, and put my hoodie on. Seals hoodie of course, my father wouldn't have it any other way. I grab a leftover hotdog and a bottle of water from the press box concessions on my way out. I take the elevator down to the concourse and wander through the now empty stadium. Seals WIN is still flashing on the big screen and light bars. The cleaning crew is beginning to sweep through methodically section by section to clean up after the fans.

I make my usual small talk with security at the employee gate and put my Air Pods in as I step out onto the sidewalk for my walk home. Tonight I'm listening to the Black Keys.

I check my surroundings as I step outside the confines of the stadium and stop in my tracks. Is that? It can't be. Why would Drew be out walking? I'm positive that's him. I'd recognize his frame anywhere. I could pick him out of a rear-view lineup any day. Especially with his confident stride. I'd heard he lives nearby. A local boy. But I didn't think it was walking distance. Maybe he's going to a restaurant? Or bar? I follow him from a distance. A block past the stadium he makes a right, then a left after 3 more blocks. I watch from the corner as his tall frame takes the steps two at a time up to the front door of a restored building from the early 1900's. The lights come on inside and I watch to see who opens the door, but he uses his own key to gain access. No one is there to greet him and he closes the door behind him. I stand there leaning on the light post as the lights throughout the home illuminate one room at a time. Shadows and figures showing in the windows, but only of one. I lose track of time and finish my walk home, only a few more blocks to the apartment I share with my roommate Caroline.

I walk through the door to Caroline sitting cross-legged on the floor watching YouTube, "Why are you so late? The game was over two hours ago."

"It takes time to get the stats reviewed and submitted, you know that," I say matter-of-factly.

She turns indignantly and stares at me, "I'm aware how

long it takes you to do things and anything involving numbers is a breeze for you. So, cut the crap."

"Maybe everything isn't as easy for me as you think it is," I reply quickly. "You know that every game isn't the same. Some have more pitches and more hits than others. That takes more time."

"Did you forget that I've been your roommate for years?"

"No."

She turns toward me, inspecting my expression, "And how many pitches and plays did this game have?"

"144 pitches and 8 hits," I reply specifically.

"And what's the average?" She asks smartly.

"The average for the league is 146 pitches, and 8.3 hits per game," I recite from memory.

"So, this was a less than average game. What took you so long?"

Think fast, "Actually the San Diego Seals average runs quite a bit different from the league overall, with only 141 pitches and 8.7 hits per game."

Caroline smirks, "And where were you? Don't try to snow me with those numbers, I took statistics and at most you're talking about a difference of five minutes in the game and that's giving you some extra benefit."

I quirk my head to the side to pretend I'm trying to remember something, "When did my mom call and have you take over her duties?"

"Ha ha," she shakes her head. "The point is that it's important that we look out for one another and have each other's back. That's impossible to do when you're gallivanting around town at all hours without notifying me where you are."

"We share our locations on our phones. You can always see where I'm at," I retort.

"Yes, but I don't want to invade your privacy. That's for emergencies."

I throw my hands up in the air and walk to my bedroom, "I love you too, Caroline. I'm going to bed."

"You mean read all night?"

"Probably."

"Goodnight."

I pull my jeans off and get comfortable in bed with my current trashy romance novel. I've got a thing for forbidden teacher-college student romance and sports romance. I fluff my pillows and adjust my reading lamp, then gather my throw pillows up around me for support while I read.

CHAPTER FOUR

Drew

I took over the family house downtown last year and I've had it completely gutted and renovated within the historical committee's standards. All new wiring and plumbing, retrofitted the structure and added central air and heat. I had piles added under the house and replaced the foundation. I also had the interior completely redesigned with touches from the era the house was built in, but with modern amenities. I moved in a month ago and I still have contractors and a designer working on the four attached apartments and potential plans for adding a cottage or two on the rear of the property.

I remember visiting my grandparents here and even though it's been cleaned up, it still holds all of the love and memories. It felt like home the day I moved in.

At first, I was concerned about walking around town and running into baseball fans. But I felt stupid driving my car four blocks to work and enjoy the walk. The cool breeze off the San Diego Bay against my cheeks and the chance to stretch out my legs. So far it hasn't been a problem. By the time I leave the stadium the fans are long gone. I've been able to call in orders for my favorite pasta and pick it up when I walk by on my way home—I'm not sure they're aware I'm a player and I like it that way.

Tonight I'm packing for the road trip to Atlanta and reviewing a book of information on the potential pitchers we will see there, as well as the plan for how we'll be pitching to their hitters, and where we should be hitting to. It doesn't work out exactly the way it's written, but we do our best. I guess I shouldn't speak for the whole team. I do my best and spend my time studying the information that's provided to me, plus I've got the last time we played them on my TV right now. I love to study the game and all of its moving parts. I want to win.

It's an early flight out in the morning. I strip down to nothing and crawl into my bed naked, ready to sleep.

CHAPTER FIVE

Maggie

I wake up with my book on top of me thinking that I need to get a pair of binoculars. I need a better look at that house Drew Brandt went into last night. Since I have the budget of a master's student that works part-time at the stadium, I go internet shopping for binoculars. Of course this sends me down a rabbit hole of research on binoculars. If I'm going to spend the money I want to make sure they will do what I want and do it well. I figure I need a clear view from at least 100 feet, and more would be better. I need to keep my distance. I'm curious. I don't want to invade his privacy. I realize this is a pawn shop mission and prepare to make my rounds in search of binoculars.

The team is away for a few days and I don't travel with the team—I have to trust the scorekeeper. I watch each of the away games from home and keep score and stats for myself. When the official scorekeeper records are available I review them, and if there's anything egregious I email the scorekeeper. He has sent me texts during the game asking for a photo of my scorebook for a specific inning, but never asking about a specific hit or stat. He'll never admit that he's not perfect. It's a good thing that he only keeps the score and not the stats. I've got the stats set up on an automated spreadsheet and I review the outcome of every play of the game as my double-check system. I do things a little different since I'm using the stats for my research as well. I keep two scorebooks, defense and offense. I need the details on every swing of the bat, but also who catches it, fumbles it, dives for it, loses it in the lights, allows it to roll between his legs, and turns a double play. Baseball players need to be well-rounded with an understanding of hitting and fielding that they demonstrate consistently on the field. Numbers don't lie, they don't say "good game" and pat you on the butt after a game when you strike out three times or commit an error.

Since it's a travel day for the team, I put it off because I have no other reason to leave the house today. I sit in my bed working on my thesis. I update my statistics and review them multiple times in search of patterns. I add notes to the appropriate places and run the data to produce updated charts. I highlight the anomalies and read through my paper to this point. Everything is on track, I need to create additional statistics that break down the cost of what each individual player does. I make a list of what needs to be included and apply values to the different things players do. I start to use Drew as my sample player before I derive numbers for each of the players, and my brain goes to mush simply envisioning his smile. I put my thesis away and snuggle back into the blankets with my forbidden hot college professor.

THE NEXT MORNING I force myself out from under my thick furry blanket and dress quickly in jeans and a T-shirt to go grab my morning coffee. I brush my hair up into a ponytail, shove my necessities into my pockets, slide into my sneakers, and head out the door. It's a two block walk to my favorite caffeine fix where I find Caroline behind the counter concocting satisfying wake up drinks.

I'm still a good fifteen feet away when she starts, "Good morning, Mags. How about a juice or smoothie to get you going this morning?"

"Coffee," I reply plainly.

"How about something fresh and healthy for a change?" She pushes.

"Coffee. Please," I try to force a smile onto my sleeping body that desperately needs caffeine.

She continues bright and cheery as she takes care of her other customers, "The vitamins would be good for you."

"I understand the science of nutrition, mother. Coffee. Please. Large. Stir in some chocolate syrup," I stare at her blankly.

"And grumpy. What's got you so grumpy this morning?" She smiles.

"The grumpy will go away when you give me my coffee. I could get my coffee elsewhere, you know," I retort without thinking in my decaffeinated state.

Caroline belly laughs, "That would cost you money and I make the best coffee in the village."

And here I pay with my pride and humiliation. Though, it's true she does make the best coffee. I glare at her in her hot pink tank top and matching headband like she's from an 80's workout video until she hands over my morning requirement, "Thank you."

"Working on your thesis today?"

"I'm out getting some errands done and I need to be home to watch the game early. The Seals are in Atlanta for a few days."

"What kind of errands?"

"Just some things I need to get done," there's no way I tell her I'm trolling pawn shops for binoculars. I need to throw her off, "Do you need me to get you anything while I'm out?" That should do it.

"Maybe grab one of those pizzas and we can watch the game together."

I nod, "Great idea." I hate it when she watches the game with me. I'm trying to concentrate and keep track of everything while she chats with me. Crap! My binoculars budget just got reduced by one pizza. Don't get me wrong. I have the best roommate, she's grown to be my best friend, and that's actually the problem—she knows me too well, but doesn't always get that I'm working or she doesn't care that she's interrupting. Probably the latter now that I think about it.

"Get the jumbo size with mushrooms, tomatoes, garlic, and Italian sausage, and a side of marinara," she adds energetically.

"Yum. I'm on it. Thanks for the coffee. See you later," I wave and turn away.

I walk to Drew's house to check it out in the daylight. The white slatted exterior is like new, the original windows clean and preserved, the trim and handrails a fresh slate gray, and the meticulous small lawn edged by flower beds bursting with vibrant pink and yellow roses. Wrought iron gates secure the expansive backyard on both sides, while the short gate to the front walkway is open and welcoming. I gaze at it from the corner and walk down the street on the opposite side, then cross and walk back up his street. I stop in front of his house, staring up at it and daydreaming about things that happen inside until I'm startled by the mailman.

I need to get on with my day anyway. I enjoy the rest of my coffee while I walk to my first stop.

Pawn shops are always a mixed bag. You could walk into treasure or trash. I step through the door and it makes a bing bong noise as I'm greeted, "Hey numbers girl. What are you looking for today?" The middle-aged man behind the counter with a Brooklyn accent says while trying to hide that he's smoking.

I smile not wanting to search for where I might find my target, "Binoculars."

"Check the third case on the left. I think I've got a few pair," he says.

"Do you know anything about them?"

He walks over to the display case and surveys the contents, "Not really. You probably want a larger pair to get a good view."

Larger means heavier and possibly harder to keep in focus, I remember from my research. "Can I see them all?" I ask wanting to try them and get an idea of what I'm searching for.

He spreads a piece of felt across the top of the display case and pulls the three pairs of binoculars out for me to try, "You take your time and let me know if you need help. I know you want to take a close look at each of them." He walks away and I wonder if I've been here too many times. He remembers who I am and how I do things. He's not wrong, my analytical side takes over often.

The first pair are a waste, plastic and probably for children. The second pair are about the size I'm looking for, but they're so dirty I'm afraid to get them near my eyes. The third pair are heavy, larger than what I was thinking of, but clear and easy to get into focus. I hold the third pair up and ask, "How much for this pair?"

"$190, but for you I can do $175. Repeat customer discount," he says.

"Okay. I'll keep them in mind. Thanks," I say as I walk out the door.

"You know where to find me. See you soon," he replies.

I never buy on my first stop and I'm hoping to find a light-weight pair that's lower cost. Onto stop two.

I walk up six blocks and make a right to get to the next pawn shop. It's a huge, busy store with three guys working there. Everyone is busy so I walk around in search of where they might keep binoculars—if they have any. I find a tele-scope that's the size I'd like to get with the bells and whistles I want and get distracted.

"The telescope is $200. $250 with the stand and extra equipment," a twenty-something guy with dark hair that's a mess nods at me from across the store.

"Thanks," I reply. "Do you have any binoculars?"

He reaches up to the shelf behind him, "Only these brass opera glasses." He flips them back and forth unsure what to do with them. "They're from the 1800's. A little scratched up but they still work."

Those wouldn't be suspicious at all, I laugh to myself, "Thanks. I'll keep the telescope in mind."

"No problem. Did you ever buy a bicycle? I've got quite a few in right now. I can make you a good deal."

"I bought a bike, thanks," I say as I walk out the door. Is it their job to remember customers or am I truly that memorable?

Short on time, I call in my pizza order so I can pick it up on my walk home and walk the couple blocks to the next pawn shop.

This place is run by an old couple and it's been here forever. I push the door open and I'm greeted by air conditioning, a freshly cleaned smell, and music from the 1950's. The woman comes out from behind the curtain in the back of the store, her gray hair sprayed into a hard helmet wearing a sheath dress adorned with a large brooch at the center of the neckline and pilgrim heels. "How are you today, dear?" She asks with a smile.

"I'm well. I'm looking for binoculars today. How are you?"

"Just old as usual," she replies happily. She surveys her store, "I have at least one pair." She walks off to a corner, "And I have these, but I think they're some kind of virtual reality goggles or something. Probably not what you want." I take the goggles from her and the internal digital display instantly lights up. They focus easily, but I don't need a new game. She hands me the pair of binoculars. They have the weight I want. I hold them up to my eyes and focus them to find that one of the lenses is badly scratched.

I hand them back to her, "These are scratched."

She puts her hands on her hips, "Sorry about that, I can sell you these crazy goggles for $100."

"I'll keep them in mind, I need to find out more about them," I take a photo of the label on the goggles so I can figure out what they are. "Have a good afternoon," I address the woman.

"You too, I hope you find what you're looking for," she waves.

I walk home taking a slight detour to pick up the pizza.

I GET HOME with less than an hour until the game starts and immediately flip on the TV and change the channel to the game. The TV comes on blaring out loud and Caroline jumps out of her skin from napping on the sofa.

"Sorry, I didn't notice you were there," I say as I get my lap desk ready. "You must've been out."

She sits there trying to recover, already changed into her oversized Seals shirt and leggings with her hot pink slouch socks still on from earlier pulled up over them. She smiles, "I smell pizza." She gets up and heads directly for the kitchen, returning with two cans of soda and the whole roll of paper towels.

I get my notes set to keep track of the game and listen to the pregame show, noting things they expect to see in the series against Atlanta.

Caroline plops down next to me and rips the pizza box into pieces to use as plates. "How's your thesis going?"

"I'm happy with it so far. I'll probably be locked in my room for weeks after the end of the season going over results and making comparisons." I laugh but it's not really funny. There's so much to be done and to be decided on for my thesis and me afterwards. It's nerve-racking when I stop and consider it all.

"I'll remember that and slide the coffee into your room quietly every morning," she chuckles.

"Maybe a straight IV drip would be better," I suggest thinking about how many hours it's all going to take and how much focus I need to have—coffee is my lifeline.

"I'll leave you a fresh thermos full every day." She stops then continues, "It's been more than a year since I graduated, I should be doing more than working at the coffee stand."

"What do you want to do? Change jobs to something that uses your degree? Go back to school?"

"I have no idea. I like working at the coffee stand."

"You do make the best coffee in the village and beyond. How can you apply your degree to the coffee stand?"

She nods but doesn't respond. We inhale the pizza while we watch the game and I do my best to keep up with scoring and stats.

CHAPTER SIX

Maggie

I get up the next morning refreshed and head out to get my coffee from Caroline. She's busy and makes faces at me the whole time but we don't exchange any words. She's probably wanting to know why I'm so early this morning. The answer is *I don't know*. I've got things to get done. I finished my current read. I need to find binoculars. I need to go to the university and check in with my department. And I need to do laundry like yesterday.

With coffee in hand I walk the mile to the next pawn shop. It gives me a vibe like it's run by a military faction or it's the front for some shady business every time I walk through the door. That doesn't stop me from exploring what it has to offer, though maybe it should. Probably not the best idea for a young woman to shop here alone. Anyway, I'm smacked in the face with the scents of sandalwood and tobacco as I survey my surroundings, for safety as well as binoculars.

A man with a head full of thick dark hair and a beard to

match welcomes me, "Can I help you find anything?" He scratches at his beard.

"Do you have any binoculars?"

"Yes! We have quite a selection of them," he replies confidently.

"Do you know anything about them?"

"I can help you out. What do you want to use the binoculars for?" He nods waiting for an answer.

An answer I'm not prepared to give. *Well, I want a better look at my crush and he just moved into my neighborhood.* Probably not. *Baseball player watching.* Has potential, but needs to be perfected. Though both sound better than *I'm not a stalker, I'm keeping my distance to give the man some privacy which is why I need binoculars that will give a clear view from at least 100 feet.* Hmmm... *Animal watching?* Technically he is an animal. I'm doing scientific research... WAIT!... "I'm working on my thesis on baseball statistics and need a better view of the players sometimes," yep, that works and I didn't even lie!

He shakes his head, "I don't think you will be happy with binoculars."

"How else will I get a more close-up view?" I glare at him confused.

He gestures at me to let him finish, "Binoculars are perfect for daytime. The stadium is lit but not the same as natural light. You could have an issue at night with a blurry or shadowed view. If you want to see across the field that's quite a distance and an obstacle on its own."

"I only need to see 100 feet or so," I blurt out without thinking.

"Oh, trying to see home plate when players score? Makes sense. There's been a ton of out calls that look safe to me, too," he nods.

Phew! "Yes, exactly," I agree quickly.

He turns around and pulls a case down off the shelf, and I prepare to duck and cover just in case. "Night vision goggles may work better for you, but depending on your angle you could catch too much light—you may need both binoculars and night vision goggles," he nods confirming. He lays the case on the counter and opens it to a pair of goggles that are exactly like those the old woman had yesterday. "Problem is, I don't have the paperwork or instructions for these."

"I do want to use the binoculars at night," I shift my stance.

He smiles, "I'll make you a deal. Buy these and give them a try." He cocks his head, "How did the earrings you bought last time work out?"

"Great! She asked me if I cleaned them for her and not another word. It was lucky that you had them become available the very next day after I stopped in searching for them," I wonder where they came from? Did they steal them or, never mind. I don't want to know. I had borrowed some beautiful gold and diamond earrings from Caroline and lost one of them. I couldn't tell her.

He nods some more, "Happy to help you with that."

I pick up the goggles to find the same label and model number as the goggles the old woman had. "How much?"

"$190 including the case," he replies.

I'm not giving this guy $90 for the case. "You don't have the instructions or any paperwork for them?"

"No. For you, I can go $150," he grins.

"They might not work. Then I'm stuck with them, my money is gone, and I still can't see the plays," I glare at him. I want to tell him I'm a student with a limited income, but I'm afraid he'd offer a pay by sexual favor option or to be my pimp.

He doesn't say anything.

"I'll think about it," also known as I'll go buy them at the other pawn shop. "Thanks," I turn and walk out of the store.

I stop a few doors down and finish the last few sips of my coffee while I look up the model number to verify they're night vision goggles. I'd never considered night vision goggles, but it makes sense. I should go back and buy them from him just for suggesting them.

I walk to the pawn shop with the old couple and I'm greeted by the couple this time. Her in an old-fashioned ivory blouse with a cameo pin and her hair tied up with a chopstick. He is in brown corduroy pants and a Seals shirt with the lighting reflecting off his bald head. "Hello dear, did you find the binoculars you were looking for?"

I smile, "I did not. Do you still have those funny goggles?"

"We do, would you like to see them?"

"Yes, please," I gaze around the safe and inviting store that smells of Ben Gay today while she retrieves the goggles.

She spreads a quilted cloth out on top of a display case and sets the goggles on it, "Take your time and get a good look at them."

I do just that. I have charging cables that fit the ports. I press the power button and the screen lights up. I have no idea what I'm doing, but I'm intrigued with new electronics. They aren't cracked and there don't appear to be any scratches on the lenses. I attempt to focus them and find that will take some practice. "How much did you say these are?"

"$100 as-is," she replies.

"Do you have a case for them or any cables or paperwork?" I ask already aware of what I'm getting and that I'm buying them.

"I can include a cable that will work with them from our

extra stock, but they were brought in just as you see them. Nothing else included," she says sweetly.

The old man pipes into the conversation, "She's such a sweet girl, give them to her for $90. Nobody else is going to want that crap."

"I'll take them," I say quickly and start digging in my wallet.

She gives her husband the side-eye scowl, "You're always giving everything away."

His mouth agape, "We only gave the guy $40 for them."

I hand them $90 cash and get out before the battle ensues.

You may think I have priority issues, but I'm giddy as a young child with a new toy to play with. I forget about the university and run home to clean my new-to-me night vision goggles and give them a try before my roommate gets home and stares at me like I'm a goon. Caroline will assume they're a virtual reality accessory for a game.

Trying to maintain my adult status, I sort my dirty clothes into half a dozen piles and get my laundry started. I clean the goggles with my electronics cleaning kit and Q-tips (yes, I'm a nerd), and take them to bed with me (Get your mind out of the gutter! What would I do with night vision goggles?), pulling the blankets up over me and attempting to create some dark (Yes, I do realize that I bought them to get under the blankets in the dark with Drew). The bedding creates a problem though (I wonder if the bedding will create a problem when we're naked together? OMG, will he insist we keep the lights on and throw the blankets on the floor? What if he's into handcuffs? Or anal!), how am I supposed to focus on something far away when I'm in an enclosed blanket fort? I get up and pull the drapes closed, close the door to my room, turn everything that produces light off, and the laundry buzzes. I stop everything, move my whites to the dryer, and load the washer with my jeans. Where was I? Oh yes, (Naked in his arms.) back to my bedroom. I put the goggles on and shut my bedroom door. It's not pitch black, but it's dark and that's all I want. I play with the focus and work my way through the menu options, then back to focusing again. All the time walking around my bedroom of laundry land-mines and books.

My bedroom door opens suddenly and I'm disoriented by the lights coming on, "What the fuck are you doing?" Caroline exclaims as my ass falls to the floor. "Are you playing a game in the dark?"

Easy answer, "Yes." I'm actually learning how to use these so I can play a game in the dark and maybe see what other games I can play with him in the dark. Oh good god! I have issues. What am I thinking? Why would he be interested in me? If he was interested in me he would've said something by now. I would think. He's a hot professional baseball player who can have about any woman he wants, he's not interested in a science nerd who can barely pay her rent some months and just bought night vision goggles so she can, ummm, observe night time activities. Specifically his night time activities and would like to find a way to become part of them. Am I a stalker? I bought equipment so I can watch him. Shit! Shit! Shit! And then I'm reminded...

"Okay, one more time... What are you doing?" Caroline asks timidly. "Why did you make your room dark in the middle of the day? Aren't you supposed to be at the university?"

Why is she so inquisitive? "I'm learning how to use these goggles." That will get her off my back. Not.

"And the goggles are for...?" She leads.

I take the goggles off, carefully placing them on my bed

and pick myself up off the ground. "I skipped university today. I needed to do laundry."

The laundry buzzes again. Saved by the laundry! I squeeze through my doorway that she's standing in and make my way to the laundry room. I methodically fold my whites with no sense of urgency and toss my jeans in the dryer, hanging the pair that will shrink. I turn to get my next pile from my bedroom and Caroline is standing in the doorway, blocking my exit.

"Excuse me, I need to get my next load," I smile and she lets me pass. I pick up my pile of dark shirts, which is most of my clothes since the Seals are navy and lime, and get that load washing.

I can't simply go back to my room and proceed with testing the goggles. She won't let it go. "Have you thought about what you can do to use your degree?"

She's silent for a moment but eventually responds "Actually, yes." She perks up with her response.

"Whatever it is, you seem happy about it," I try to be encouraging.

"I'm thinking about buying the coffee stand."

"What?" My eyes about pop out of my head.

"I like it there and I like making coffee. What better way to use my business degree than to own a business?"

"Wow. I didn't know it was for sale?"

"Everything is for sale if the offer is right. I need to work on the numbers to see what the cost would be to open a new stand from scratch, then prepare an offer to buy the existing stand."

"That's your business degree at work, and you can make the updates you've talked about but the boss won't let you do."

"Yes. Plus, the goal would be to create a turnkey business

and offer franchises," she smiles satisfied with herself. "Makes me happy and just think of all the people on the planet that would be happy with the 'best coffee.'"

I grin, "Truly making the planet a better place."

Caroline laughs.

"You should call it 'Sweet Caroline's' and add those little biscuit cookies you bake."

"Yes! Great idea." She disappears to the other room, I can only assume to make some notes on her business plan.

I turn the knob on the dryer back to the beginning so I don't have to drop everything to run it again in fifteen minutes. Jeans always take two rounds of the dryer. I peek in on Caroline in her room to find her with her glasses on in front of her laptop. I haven't seen much of that since she graduated. "Ahem, I'll be in my room if you need me," I nod, anxious to get back to my goggles.

"Cool," she replies without breaking away from her screen and I hurry off to my room before she changes her mind.

Once I'm in the dark and have the goggles on, I stand in one corner of my room and slowly scan from one side of my room to the other attempting to get the hang of these things. The size of my room is limiting even at the lowest level of zoom. I notice something moving in the corner, as big as my face and it appears to be furry. What the fuck is that? I attempt to back up, but I'm already in the corner and stumble with nowhere to go. The furry blob is coming down from the ceiling. Is there something there or am I somehow seeing an apparition floating that wasn't visible without the goggles? It stops moving. Still, simply breathing at my eye level. Which is better than I can say for myself, I can't breathe and it's as if I'll never blink again. It turns but stays where it's at. I pull the goggles off quickly and flip the light on, trying to focus with the lighting change. There's nothing there. Science doesn't lie and there was definitely something there for the night vision goggles to show it, they don't have the capability to create things—at least I hope they don't.

I send Caroline a text:

Me: If I'm not out of my room in the next five minutes, get out, lock the door behind you, and don't come back without a hazmat suit and a big dumb man to protect you.

There's no reason to waste a smart man, they're so limited in numbers as it is. I shove my phone in my pocket and it dings at me incessantly. I ignore it and walk slowly toward the corner with the furry blob. There's obviously not an extra-terrestrial resembling a tribble the size of my head in my room. Where would it hide? Where could it have gone so quick? What if it changes shape? Or shrinks? Or, worse, gets bigger? What if it ate the whole building, and our apartment along with all of our neighbors is in its stomach right now? I storm the last 4 steps to where the monster appeared to be and find myself standing in front of my chain of plushies that is hanging from the ceiling. Is one of them alive? Possessed? I don't think that's possible unless we're in Dr. Frankenstein's laboratory or someplace similar. Who would bring a plushie to life?

Standing facing the corner of my room, Caroline comes rushing in, slamming the door open, "Are you okay? What's going on?"

"SShhhhh!" She stands in the doorway staring at me.

"Are you standing in the corner to punish yourself? Were you a bad girl?" She chuckles.

I turn and glare at her and then focus on the corner in

front of me to come face to face with a beady-eyed hamster, "Damn it, Frank! I thought you'd left me. How long have you been in here?" I reach my hand out and he crawls into it and up my arm to my shoulder.

Caroline sighs exasperated, "Better questions would be, *Where has he peed?* and *What has he eaten?*"

"Oh you're right," I reply quickly and walk to the kitchen to find him some food and fill his water bottle.

"That's not what I meant," she confirms.

"Don't worry, he's been in my room."

"I guess that's something. Are you in need of my rescue services any longer this evening?" she asks sarcastically.

"Oh, no. I think we're fine."

Frank is not as big as my head, but at the minimal distance and zoom he could appear to be. I need to take my goggles outside.

It's still light out. I take a snack and Frank back to my bedroom and grab the next book off the top of my to-be-read pile. I get comfortable with Frank snuggled up next to me on my pillow and settle in to read a boy-next-door romance. I'm happy to find that it's something lighter after my heart-stopping invasion.

CHAPTER SEVEN

Drew

We have one more game left against Atlanta before we head home from the quick road trip. The team is on a tear and seems to keep getting better, but I'd never say that out loud.

Since I moved into my house I'm finding I dislike road trips. There's something about having a home where I belong, that's part of the family. A place where I belong.

CHAPTER EIGHT

Maggie

I'd forgotten what it was like to live with a business major instead of a happy-go-lucky barista. It's time for the last away game of the road trip and I picked up a pizza exactly the way she likes it on the way home from the university. I get the pizza set on the coffee table, box torn into pieces to use as our plates and grab us a couple sodas. No Caroline. I get my notes ready and all my colored pencils for scorekeeping and stats. Still no Caroline.

"Caroline?" I call out.

"Yea?" Mumbles from her bedroom.

"Pizza," I call out happily.

"Okay," but there's no movement.

I watch the pregame show and make some notes.

"Pizza is getting cold," I call out again.

"Pizza?"

"I brought home your favorite pizza," I reiterate.

Caroline joins me in the living room, "Why didn't you

tell me?" She gets comfortable with her foot tucked under her on the couch and shoves a slice in her mouth with her laptop still open on her lap. She doesn't say another word throughout the whole game. I'm not sure she's breathing, she hasn't taken her nose out of her laptop.

I'm accustomed to multi-tasking. Keeping score, making notes on plays, tracking stats, chatting with Caroline, and watching the game all at the same time. Without Caroline in the mix, I find myself distracted by other things, or I should say someone else. I've had a crush on him since way before he had his professionally honed physique. I remember when he was tall, skinny, and gangly. He didn't have any shoulder mass at all. Seriously, he would've been the one they sent to army crawl through the narrow passage or air conditioning vents because he's the only one who would've fit. Now his shoulders are sexy and top off his V-shaped torso like they've always been there. His biceps have developed from his spaghetti arms to sexy masses of cut muscle, as have his calves and thighs and ass. His eyes, however, have stayed exactly the same—always warm and friendly. I could melt into his eyes. I imagine his lips are soft and inviting. I daydream about him often. The warmth of his hands on me. The heat of his body against mine. The tenderness of his breath at my ear. His manly scent invading my senses. Wetting his lips with his tongue as he leans in to kiss me, holding me against him as he claims me completely as his. He releases me, dragging his hand down my arm and entwining his fingers with mine, holding my hand tightly. He stops and smiles at me, a knowing smile, and my heart beats stronger simply from the vision of his smile. I catch myself giggling and I'm happy that Caroline is preoccupied, instead of all over me with questions. It's the eighth inning and my notes stopped in the fifth. The batter hits the ball and Drew grabs it on a bounce, throwing it to Martin at first getting yet another double play and ending the inning. The satisfaction and intensity on his face is a rush and sexy as hell. Yet, I still remember the teenager that I originally fell for. Okay, I guess fell for may not quite be the correct terminology, but there's been nobody for me but him since I first saw him play. I don't care that he's a major leaguer. I'd want to be with him if he was flipping burgers and playing in a recreational league—but he's always had drive and goals. And at least in my head, he's always had heart.

The game was over and I didn't even notice the end. I gather my papers and pencils, and go to my room to find Frank cozy in my bed gnawing on the cover of my current read. I move him over and climb in bed, falling asleep with thoughts of Drew and hoping for dreams of us together.

It's a long day when you wake up early and don't start work until 6pm. I take advantage of the morning to read the baseball news and get caught up on trends that are happening around the league, mostly in search of things I could include in my statistics and thesis. I plug in my night vision goggles to get them fully charged and get caught up on my stats before I need to walk to the stadium. I take the time to review the scorekeeper's notes and update what I missed. I chart some numbers that catch my eye and leave them for later, deciding to rest my eyes and brain for a bit before work.

Refreshed, I pack up my backpack as usual but add the night vision goggles. We're going on a test run tonight.

. . .

IT WAS A SHITTY GAME. You don't win them all and we lost this one 0-7. Not only were we unable to score, but the ball was finding places to get stuck in the wall and hitting the corners of the bases in a way that would cause it to bounce unpredictably. Like the whole batch was weighted off-center, of course they weren't. The play of the game was the visiting team, and that never happens.

Regardless, I go through my process reviewing the numbers, chatting with the scorekeeper, updating stats, and submitting it all to the management team. I sit for a moment gazing at the field. It's peaceful and quiet, a stark contrast to the divisive chants and cat calls of an hour ago.

I pack up my stuff and start my journey home through the stadium to the employee exit. I wonder if I'll see Drew walking home again tonight. I'm going to try my goggles tonight, but I don't want anyone to see me. Maybe I should find another place to try them out? Or maybe I should just put them on and wear them for the walk home? That's not suspicious at all.

No sign of Drew. I walk to the corner of his street and find the lights are already on at his house. I stand still waiting for a sign that he's home and the lights aren't on for some other reason. I walk closer and get my night vision goggles out, leaning on a neighbor's tree for stability. "Here we go," I say to myself and hit the power button. A bright white screen flashes in my eyes, about blinding me. I take a deep breath and regain my focus, refusing to let it disorient me again. Slowly, I turn my head to get my bearings and attempt to decipher which direction I'm facing and what I'm focused on. I dial the telephoto lens back as far as I can and adjust the focus until there's a distinctive form. I take the goggles off and step up onto a rock trying to gain a few inches of height for a better view and not wanting to increase the zoom. Baby steps. I need to get these things to work. Balanced on the rock I put my goggles back on and reach out for something to hold onto, though there's nothing within my reach. These things throw off my depth perception. There's a figure in his window, the drapes pull back and it's him. He opens the window and the curtains blow in the breeze around him. There's music wafting from his home, a soft and gentle yet yacht rockish melody. I wonder if he'd take me in his arms and dance with me? Twirling me around the room with his confident ease. His warm hand possessively at the small of my back holding me against him as he guides me, gliding about so smoothly it's as if we're floating and the room is spinning around us. He's no longer at his window but the warmth of his home is obvious and inviting. Should I walk up to the front door and knock? Forget about the goggles and the binoculars. And say what? *Hi, I've been stalking you for over 10 years now. Want to date me?* Probably not. Maybe I should leave a note on his door inviting him to coffee? But I couldn't take him to the best coffee because—well, Caroline. There's nowhere to sit there anywhere. I hope she fixes that when she takes it over. I need to suggest that. I could use the approach I used when I was younger, *Hi, would you like to buy some girl scout cookies?* Also not the vibe I want to give. I'm not a child, though I still love girl scout cookies. I wonder if I have any thin mints left in the freezer. Suddenly something rustles in the bushes and scampers over my feet. I'm brought back to reality as I find myself lying in a bush with a squirrel filling his cheeks. His door flies open and he calls out, "Everything okay out there?" I stay silent and still. He won't find me in a bush 2 doors down and luckily there's nobody here to witness my embarrassment.

I get up trying to avoid the prickles of the bush while the squirrel seems to watch and laugh with a clicking sound. "I'm going to tell Frank about you," I scold quietly. I gather myself and peep through the bushes to be sure Drew's not watching. The coast is clear, so I do my best impersonation of a ninja and head home.

———

CAROLINE IS SHUT in her room and I go directly to mine. Putting away my things I glance in the mirror and find leaves in my hair, I'm also reminded that the lime piping on my Seals jacket glows. So not a ninja.

CHAPTER NINE

Maggie

I'm nothing if not persistent and logical. I can figure this out. It's not the goggles just like it's not the computer or the software, it's got to be user error. I hate to admit it, but it's not my fault they didn't come with a manual. I'd have read it from front to back twice and tried different modes following the step-by-step instructions it included. But that's not how this is going down. I found the manual online, unfortunately it's not in English, Spanish, or any other language I could attempt to decipher—I have no idea where to start with kanji. I did, however, find some instructional videos for a similar model and set up my night vision goggles for what my desired use is (surveillance is what they call it, but that's *their* terminology). So, I'm ready to give it another try. But first I'm going to do some daytime reconnaissance. I'm not going to end up in the same position I was in last night with no clue what is in my line of sight. I'm going to be overly aware of everything around me on purpose and more than just things that could threaten my personal safety.

Huh, funny that I didn't consider safety when I walked into the pawn shop that has always given me the heebie jeebies.

Drew would never hurt me. Then again, would he? My heart is his and I'm not sure he even knows my name. I wasn't talking about heartbreak when I said personal safety, but now I'm wondering if I should be considering that. He could totally wreck me and hurt me more than anybody else. What's worse? I'll let him. I'd rather have my chance than regret never taking it. I'd be hurting myself more if I didn't take the chance and closed myself off from the risk of love. I suppose that's not up to me though if he's not interested. And it's not like we're dating or talk to each other—ever. Technically we work at the same place, so I suppose we're co-workers which throws another wrench in the works because employers tend to frown on dating in the workplace. I'm sure baseball players get special privileges. Statisticians probably don't and are replaceable. Jobs that provide me with information I need for my thesis are hard to come by. I really need to rethink my choices.

I wonder what the statistics are on the risk of love? There's got to be numbers on that somewhere. It could make for an interesting thesis and a good basis for a dating service to use in creating a match algorithm that would get better and better as more information was fed into it. You know, law of large numbers and all. I wonder what the quantitative numbers are for the factors of love and human emotions. Can human emotions even be assigned consistent variables to work with to create successful formulas and matches? Everything has a value in statistics. Caroline and I should open a matchmaking service right after she gets her coffee shop franchised and I complete my masters.

I stop as I put my hoodie on to walk out the door on my reconnaissance mission and realize I have a problem: The risk I'm taking for a man. Worse yet, it's not stopping me.

I take a walk around the neighborhood observing the details that I've not given any consideration to until now. A bus stop with a shelter at the corner. A concrete table hidden in the garden of the yard a few doors down from his. The upstairs patio of the brewery on the corner would have a great view, probably not night vision goggles friendly.

Old homes intermingled with apartment buildings and restaurants on the end of the blocks. The plain buildings painted with bright colored murals and the old homes maintained to their original glory to preserve history. It's a unique area and I love it here. Where else can you go to the baseball game, out to eat, the pawn shop, grab coffee, get groceries, and live all within a few blocks?

I think I'll get a better view from the other side of the house. I nod to myself with a new plan established and go home for a nap before the game.

THE WAY the sun shines through my window is nap inducing. I stretch, then curl up in a warm ball, allowing the warmth to lull me into a daydream.

> *Sitting in the stands at the stadium as a spectator with no score or stats to keep, just the game to enjoy. Drew glances my direction with a friendly grin and winks at me from his position at second base. I giggle to myself, but I'm sure I imagined it. What if I didn't? I'm a*

young intelligent woman. I don't have any hideous deformities or scars. I don't dress to show my figure often, never for the game, but I have one. He's bent over with his hands resting on his knees and relaxed, observing as the pitching coach throws batting practice and occasionally picking the ball when it's hit to his zone. Gorgeous and light on his feet in his heather grey cut-off sweatpants and a T-shirt that the sleeves have been ripped off of. His Seals cap shading his face and helping his Oakley's with the glare of the bright after-noon sun. I'm stuck on how his muscular shoulders span beyond his shirt and his grey sweat shorts outline his ... cup? Is he wearing a cup? If he's not and it doesn't appear that he is, that's a package worth unwrapping. He reaches down to adjust, definitely no cup, and lifts his chin in my direction. My face warms, I'm probably turning red with embarrassment. Do you think he caught me watching him adjust his (I'm guess-ing) hard cock? If it's not hard, he's a shower not a grower. I'd be worried it would hang out of my shorts. I can't get past the outline of his cock in his grey sweats. I love baseball pants, especially when they're worn with a snug fit. But men simply shouldn't be allowed to wear sweatpants or basketball shorts outside of their home. I'm not saying it's inappropriate. It's just that, well, it distracts people and causes them to lose their ability to think clearly and perform common tasks. And by people, I mean smart women like myself. It's almost as bad as a perfectly cut adonis belt which Drew has as well. I wonder which parts of him are holding those shorts up? I rustle in my seat trying not to get my wet panties in a bunch and focus on batting practice. He walks toward first base, and me, on his way to the back-

stop. He stops briefly in front of me, swiping his thumb across his lower lip. He turns his head towards me but then keeps walking. What I wouldn't do for an up-close glimpse of his eyes, but today they're covered by his sunglasses and hiding whatever thoughts he's having. I hope I'm in his thoughts. He's a thinker like me, and quiet. We'd be perfect together if we could learn how to communicate. We'd sit on the sofa together in a spooning sort of way, each deep into a book. Me deeply engrossed in one of my taboo romances or possibly the updated baseball rules book or latest copy of the Journal of Statistical Science, and him a history book, the latest fictional spy thriller novel, or if he's in a studious mood the report on the next team the Seals will be playing. We'll share a blanket over our feet and he'll have his arm around me. No words neces-sary to be together and happy. He's standing behind the backstop now, spinning his bat end on the ground. When it's his turn to bat he swings the bat around as he walks into the batting cage and gazes in my direction when he puts his helmet on. That's the second time this afternoon. I turn around to find out who's sitting around me. Does he have a girl here? Or family visit-ing? Sitting behind me maybe? But there's only me and a couple of the old sports writers sitting anywhere nearby. Maybe it is me. Oh, I get it, he has questions about his stats or wants to schmooze me to make his numbers better. First, I wouldn't do that. Second, he may have questions, but he'd never cheat, it's simply not in his DNA. He's one of the most ethically moral men I've met. Then again, all I know is what I see on the field. He takes his swing, connecting and sending a grounder up the middle. Then swats one down the foul line into left field. He doesn't bite on the next two pitches and I swear he focuses in my direction again. Did he just point at me? He swings with everything he has on the next pitch and sends the ball out of the park. Drew steps out of the batting cage, tosses his bat and helmet to the side and walks directly toward me. Stopping just on the other side of the net from me.

He takes his sunglasses off and smiles, "Margaret? Right?"

My whole body heats up at the sight of his eyes. Blue pools deeper than a lake that a girl could dive right into. I nod, "I go by Maggie now." He remembers my name. Why didn't I just agree with him?

"I like that," his eyes shine. "Why don't I see you at batting practice more often?"

"It's not part of my job."

He quirks his head, "Why today?"

"Sometimes I need baseball to be fun, not work."

He grins again and his face lights up, "I get that. Maybe we can go to the batting cages sometime and have some fun."

Did he just ask me out on a date? "I've never been."

"You'll love it," he leans into the net and I mimic his motion.

"I'm in," I say gazing into his eyes, wanting him to kiss me and not caring one bit about the batting cages. He curls his fingers into the net and my hands meet his without a second thought. He pulls me closer to the net, licking his lower lip. He leans in. He's finally going to kiss me. I've waited so long for this. I've imagined his lips on mine so many times, but I've never gotten to experience it. I need it to confirm the chem-

istry is there between us, and I believe it is whole-heartedly.

I get a tickle on my nose and rub it to find Frank snuggled into me by my mouth and nose cooing contently. If he wasn't so soft and sweet I'd be upset. Hopefully I'll get the kiss next time.

CHAPTER TEN

Maggie

Eighty-one home games in six months can be tiring for everyone involved, but it's all about the numbers. When you think about the grind the team goes through, it's truly a feat. One hundred and sixty-two games plus traveling in a matter of about one hundred and eighty-three days. Anybody else would be starting legal action against their employer for overworking them. Twenty-one days off in six months isn't even a single day off each week. I shouldn't be complaining about my home game schedule. I watch the away games, but that's for my research.

I drag myself out of bed and get ready to go to the game. Should I be leaving early and going to batting practice? No, that was a daydream. He doesn't know I exist. No need to invest more into him than I already am, plus it'll look worse and he'll be sure I'm a stalker if he's suddenly finding me at batting practice and with night vision goggles outside of his house. Who am I kidding? The night vision goggles alone could get me arrested for any number of things and potentially branded a stalker. I block out the negativity and go on with my day. I'll go early and catch up on baseball news from the safety of my desk in the press box.

The game is a wild one... Our ace is pitching tonight and the opposing team has their number one on the mound as well. For the most part it's strike outs and pop flies throughout the game. The coaches are on top of it and supporting their players. Each time there's action they get it reversed with a challenge. Base hit? Nope. You're out. Home run? Try again, fan interference. It wasn't until the eighth inning when both starting pitchers were pulled from the scoreless game that things started to get interesting. Statistically speaking, I expect to see 8 hits in the game, but you have to consider the stats are an average. So, you will get games with twenty hits and games with none. It all balances out.

The bases are loaded with Seals and the team Captain, Seno, is at the plate. Bottom of the eighth inning with one out and the San Francisco team scored two in the top of the inning. There's history between these two teams, especially Seno and their first baseman. Seno swings with everything he's got and misses. Everybody tags up and takes a few steps off the bases, ready to run. The next pitch is outside. Seno lets loose on the next one but hits the ball off the end of the bat and it gets caught at the wall in centerfield. Cross on third tags up and his speed allows him to score. Mason tags up on second and goes for third, but gets tagged out. The coach challenges the call, but I'm not sure why. From my vantage point he was obviously out, but there must've been something odd about the play because it took the higher ups forever to review it. I took the time to indulge in a sundae from the press box concessions while waiting on the challenge. He was still out. I'm a Seals fan and will always give them the benefit of the doubt. I can still be fair and I'm right here watching the game. They should just ask me, I'd get them an answer quicker and it would have saved me some hot fudge calories.

Bottom of the ninth inning, Lucine on third base and Martin gets the intentional walk. Brandt walks up to the plate and there's visible communication between Martin and Drew. Martin takes a huge lead off first base. First pitch and it's a fast ball straight down the middle, Martin is off as soon as the ball leaves the pitchers hand and Drew lays off the gimme pitch, moving Martin to second with his steal. The next two pitches are wide outside, followed by one so far inside that he jumps back to avoid getting hit by the ball. It's all part of the game, team strategies can get into the mental game. Drew smiles, shakes his head and steps back into the batter's box.

CHAPTER ELEVEN

Drew

Come on give me that heat again. I'm not falling for the pitch inside. I'm not afraid of you. I've got Martin where I want him. A double to win this game with a walk off. We need a win. We aren't losing again. That's not what this team is about. We're going all the way this season and nobody is going to stop us. Just pitch already. Anything I can bloop over the first baseman and down the right field line would be preferred. I step out of the box and grab some clay, rubbing it in my hands while I glance up at Martin who's standing confidently in the base path already halfway to third base. He changes tactic and walks back to second, nodding at me. Lucine on third base dusts his hands off on his pants as he acknowledges he's aware we've got something going on. Martin and I have been in tune with each other all season on the bases, in fact the stats say we're the number two duo in the league for double plays. We want to be number one. When the Skipper switched up the line up and I started hitting after him we committed to taking advantage of our connection on the base paths. The team is tight, but there are some of us who are more connected than others and in our case we've decided to use it. I don't know how else to explain it, I trust my teammates with 100% of their ability but with Martin it's 100% of our ability. It's a tighter connection, we get each other. I take my time getting back in the batter's box, since they're playing a game with me now. The pitcher asking for a new ball and delaying as long as he can before he gets back on the mound. They can try to throw off my timing and concentration all they want. It's not going to happen. I'm not new to the game and I'm not a kid that distraction methods work on. It works for me and shows they underestimate me. You should never underestimate me. It's a 3-1 count and I want to finish this game, not load the bases. I stretch swinging my bat as I dig into the batter's box. The pitcher gets ready, hiding the ball behind his back. Coach is signaling me to take the pitch, wanting me to walk on ball four. But Martin is grinning like a fool and he has a view of how the pitcher is holding the ball. The pitch comes flying at me and there's no time to think. I read the pitch and smack it, sending it over the second baseman's head and bouncing in the gap between center and right field. I toss my bat and run to first, I can't make it to second and it doesn't matter because Rock has already scored and Martin was close behind him. Seals win. That's all that matters.

Suddenly I'm shocked by the freezing cold bucket of Gatorade dumped over my head. The one thing I will never get used to and I will never complain about—even when I'm cold and sticky.

I run into the locker room to shower off quickly and avoid the on-field interview. Let them talk to the pitchers in the press room. I don't need the attention.

Skip grabs me after the postgame, "Nice hit. I told you to take the pitch. I'm happy with what you did. Good trusting your gut."

"Martin's gut. He called the pitch from second base," I'll never take credit from anyone.

"It took both of you to make it happen. We are nothing without our team," he smiles and walks away.

He's right. If we've learned nothing else this season, we are better as a team or duo than alone. Martin helps me with that in baseball, but it makes it more obvious that it's missing in other aspects of my life. Moving into my family house and living there alone has brought other desires to my attention. It's too much room for just me, too quiet. I need companionship in my life. Maybe it's time to date and not be completely consumed by baseball. I'm not sure I can do that. My life is baseball and what I can do to get better at it. I've ignored women and told myself that I don't have time for things like that. Women, all relationships, take time and some are more complicated than others. Yes, I have thought about it. I overthink and analyze everything before I do it, unless I'm on the baseball field, because that's just natural to me and probably why it's where I'm happiest. I'm lucky I get to spend time there and that I've made it to where I am. The fact that I'm doing it in my hometown of San Diego is a bonus that I'm thankful for and hope doesn't change.

I'm out of the stadium for the night quicker than normal. I enjoy my walk home in the evening, it's my transition time from work to home and somehow freeing.

The lights all come on automatically when I approach, welcoming me home. I take the front steps two at a time and unlock the door. I'm happy to be home, but lonely at the same time.

CHAPTER TWELVE

Maggie

Leaving the stadium I've got my mission outlined in my head. I'm concerned that I'll be ahead of him since I was quick getting my numbers calculated and submitted. Primarily being a pitcher's duel, the few hits and plays took no time at all to get submitted. I take the long way and walk up to his house from the opposite direction. I don't like it because the walk is inefficient, adding a block and a half to my walk, but as I approach I find the lights are already on—he's home. The windows aren't open. There's no music billowing out. I watch for his figure in the window with my goggles focused and functioning, no worries of tripping or falling or grabbing onto something non-existent to steady myself. I stand on the bus bench, leaning on the neighbor's fence and supporting the weight of the night vision goggles on it. I wait and watch patiently. But there's nothing interesting. The lights all go out at once and I go home for the night.

CHAPTER THIRTEEN

Drew

"Sorry, I'm running late this morning," Martin says grinning from ear to ear as he walks into the workout room. "Surprise visitor."

"Same woman?" I ask.

"Yep. Only woman," he replies confident.

"I've never seen you with a woman," I say questioning.

"Nobody has and it's going to stay that way," he says with finality.

"Can I at least get her name?"

"Nope. That's top secret." He focuses on me, "You're a different story and obviously in need of some female companionship."

"I'm not interested in a woman who stops by for sex whenever she wants."

"Don't think for a second that's what I have. My relationship is complicated. It's worth it when you find the one you belong with. Anybody have your attention?"

"It's only been on my mind since I moved into the house. I've been thinking about what I want."

"Spill it, maybe I can help you find her. Assuming it's a her."

I sigh, "It's a her."

"I was kidding with you! Give me the specs."

I consider my words, "I don't want a woman that's interested in me because I'm a baseball player. I don't want a younger woman, at least not more than a year or two younger than me. I want a woman with goals who won't be satisfied being a housewife. If it was possible, I'd choose someone who knew me before I was a professional athlete."

"So, you want an overthinking square who's just like you. Nonsmoker. No drugs. Family oriented, but not baby crazy. Levelheaded. Quiet and easy to be around woman. Who magically existed before your baseball career and isn't influenced by it at all? Sound right?" Martin nods wide-eyed waiting for my response.

"Overthinking square isn't a requirement, but the rest," I nod in agreement.

"She doesn't exist." Martin turns in a circle, "You grew up around here, went to school not too far from here?"

"Yea, so?"

"Do you have any old friends from school or your neighborhood who have potential?"

I'd never considered it. "I don't know. It's been a long time since I've talked to any of those people."

"It's the only way to get what you want. You've got to go back to the time when you didn't worry about why people wanted to be part of your life."

"I'll think about it."

"Okay, and when you're finished thinking about it and

then overthinking it let me know. I figure that will take at least a month," Martin chuckles.

"It'll work itself out." I shake my head, "You want to go for a run?"

"Yep. Meet you in the locker room in 10 minutes."

I nod and walk down the hallway to my locker to change my shoes.

"Brandt?" Carter, the locker room manager, calls my name out as I walk by his office.

"Yea?"

"Don't waste time. Do you have your yearbooks? Or a list of classmates from your high school and junior high school years?"

"I'm sorry?"

"I heard you talking to Martin. He can be a dumbass, but he's right. I'm trying to cut the overthinking part of the process out."

"I have all of my yearbooks."

"Give them a skim. See who stands out," he smiles at me. "Listen to me, don't be alone and miserable unless you want to be."

I nod, "Thank you."

Standing under a hot shower after my run, everything becomes clear to me.

I get ready for batting practice and kick back on the sofa in the locker room with my phone to call my mom, but think better of it, not needing more of my teammates to get involved. So I send a text.

Me: Hi mom. How are you today?

Mom: Better now. Thank you. I haven't heard from you in a week.

Me: It gets busy during the season.

Me: Do you have my yearbooks?

Mom: Yes.

Mom: Why do you want them?

Mom: You don't need to be rekindling any fires with that Suzanne you dated in high school.

Mom: And the neighbor girl who swam in your kiddie pool with you got married last summer so you missed out on her.

Do not engage. Do not engage.

Me: I'm just trying to find an old friend.

Mom: A female friend.

Mom: That Johnna girl who was on the boy's basketball team with you in high school was sweet.

Me: Johnna? You mean Johnny?

Mom: The super tall girl with the long hair.

Me: Johnny, mom. Not a girl.

Mom: Oh, are you sure?

Me: Yes, mom.

Mom: My friend's daughter Becky is about your age and very nice. I can set you up on a date.

Me: I just want my yearbooks please.

Mom: Well, I'll drop them off for you when I go out to the grocery store later. Have you bought groceries for your pantry yet? You need to have staples in your kitchen cabinet.

Me: I haven't been home much.

Mom: Don't worry honey. I'll take care of that too. It'll all be done already when you get home from work tonight.

Me: Thanks mom. I can always get you tickets for the game whenever you want to go.

Mom: I know dear. You don't need your mother at your work.

Me: I've told you it's not like that. You're always welcome.

Mom: Who was the tall thin girl who kept score for your team in high school? Pretty girl. Studious. Dressed a bit on the tomboy side. Oh! My grandkids would be gorgeous!

Me: Okay. I've got to get to batting practice.

Me: Thanks mom.

Maybe I don't need my yearbooks after all. I just needed my mom.

———————

I GET HOME after the game to find my yearbooks from junior high through college stacked neatly and in chronological order on my dining room table with post-it notes marking some pages. A note from my mom on top of the pile:

Drew,

I left some notes for you in your yearbooks. I see that Suzanne wrote her number in there, please don't call her. So many wonderful pictures of you and your friends all wrote such nice things about you. I wish I would've read them sooner. I didn't find Johnna. Was Margaret Hamilton the scorekeeper girl? Your pantry is full and organized. I made sure to get your favorite snacks.

Love,

Mom

Me: Thank you mom.
Me: How much were the groceries?
Mom: Don't worry about it honey. I wanted to make sure you have everything you need. I got you the nice containers for your dry goods. Love what you've done with the house. Consider it your housewarming gift.
Me: Thanks mom.

I'm scared to see what she's done to my pantry, but anything would be better than empty. I open the cabinet, it's neat and organized with everything anyone could need for baking or a quick meal. My favorite cookies and crackers. A whole set of spices and herbs, and a selection of shelf-stable goods that work well with my travel schedule.

I grab a few cookies and sit down with my yearbooks, reading through the notes from my mom.

Don't call her.
Do you know this girl? She's pretty.
I love your smile in this photo.

*Her red hair and your blue eyes would make beautiful
grandbabies.*
This one looks high maintenance.
It's so nice to see photos of you with your friends.
*We need to find this photo and have it framed. Your
first championship win.*
Why don't I remember you running track?
*Which of the girls in the choir photo were you
there for?*
Does Suzanne have a twin sister?
*Margaret Hamilton is always around the team photos.
I'm sure she's the scorekeeper.*
*Look at the sweet note Margaret wrote in your
yearbook!*

She always has my best interest at heart. It's a start. The
quick journey down memory lane through my mom's eyes
has been enough for one night.

CHAPTER FOURTEEN

Maggie

After the game, I try a repeat of last night and hope for more activity. I get to the corner and the lights in his house are already on. There's no movement, music, open windows, shadows, or anything, but the lights are still on. I get comfortable in the bus shelter and keep watch for anything interesting. Finally there's movement in a window on the second floor, the figure takes his clothes off and disappears. Then he's in the next room and he's in the shower. He's in the shower? He's naked! I'm officially going to jail. He stands in the shower with his head tilted back. Then he lathers some soap up all over his body, obviously reaching down to pay attention to his undercarriage. He rinses off, then washes his hair and rinses off again. The window revealing enough to raise my curiosity and give away his actions. He disappears again and the lights all go off shortly after.

I step down off the bus bench and put my goggles in my backpack. My short walk home filled with images of Drew.

I walk through the front door almost short of breath, with intent to go directly to my room, but Caroline stops me, "What's the infatuation with the bus shelter, Mags? I'm that bad that you rather sit in a bus shelter than come home?"

I shake my head, "What?"

"You've been taking a long time to get home from the stadium, so I checked on you. I don't get it. Why are you avoiding me?"

"I'm not avoiding you."

"Then why don't you come home?"

"I have things to do."

She glares at me funny, "And why is your face red? Why does it look like you have rings around your eyes?"

"What are you talking about?"

"Seriously red."

"Maybe the cool breeze chapped my cheeks. You know I sit there in the press box with the breeze off the bay blowing in my face for hours some days."

"Okay, and your explanation for the rings around your eyes?"

"Well, I haven't been sleeping well. Dark circles are not an uncommon occurrence for college students. I'm sure you remember those days."

"Try again. These are not those type of circles. Why am I getting the same feeling as when you tried to hide a hickey?"

Fuck. Fuck. Fuck. "I don't know."

She stares at me sideways and doesn't say a word.

"Okay, well I'm going to get some sleep and try to get rid of these dark circles. Goodnight."

"Not so fast." Caroline walks around me like a shark

circling me. "Why does your backpack look heavier than normal?"

"I think it's the same. I'm tired, probably the way I'm holding it with no energy."

"And it's unzipped. You never walk home with your backpack unzipped." She reaches for the zipper and finds the backpack is heavier. She reaches in and pulls out my night vision goggles. "So, you take these to work? I didn't think you had time for games at work."

"I use them on my way home," well at least it's the truth. Why does she always make me feel like she's going to ground me?

Her eyes get wide, "Margaret Mae Hamilton! Those aren't game goggles are they?"

"I suppose that depends on what game you're playing," I reply flippantly.

"What game are you playing?"

Damn it. "Learn how to use night vision goggles in surveillance mode."

She turns and walks away, then walks back, "And what or who are you watching?"

"It doesn't really matter."

"Where do you have your bail money hidden?"

"Goodnight Caroline." I turn and go to my room, not wanting to continue the conversation.

I close the door behind me and climb into bed, my brain filled with visions of Drew. I turn my lights out and fall asleep hoping for dreams of me entangled with his warm naked body.

CHAPTER FIFTEEN

Drew

W hy is the name Margaret Hamilton so familiar? I wonder while I take some extra time at home this morning and make myself some coffee. Thank you mom. I grab a few cookies from my stocked pantry for dunking.

I go back to my yearbooks and flip through my mom's notes to the pages with Margaret on them to take a closer look. She was there all the way through junior high, high school, and college. Her hair always pulled up in a tight ponytail, but not up high like the cheer squad. She wears jeans or shorts, but neither are ever too tight. And she's proudly sporting a team shirt or hoodie. I find the note she wrote to me in my senior yearbook:

Drewby,
Senior year has been amazing and hectic. Maybe we
can hang out this summer? See you next year in
college.
XXOO Margaret

Drewby. I haven't heard that in years. It's a play on my nickname and last initial *Drew B*. Back then, friends were still calling me Andrew. Drewby was a team thing.

Why don't I remember this girl who was obviously in my circle?

I push my yearbooks aside and focus on the coach's report for tonight's game.

Martin: Are you at the stadium?
Me: Not yet.
Martin: Do me a solid, wait until we have to be there today so it looks like we've been working out together this morning?
Me: The woman?
Martin: Yes.
Me: Can I meet her?
Martin: Hopefully someday. Not now.
Me: Pick me up on your way in.
Martin: Perfect.

I don't have a clue what Martin is doing, but if it makes him happy I'll support it. I get my workout in at home and wait for Martin to pick me up.

MARTIN PULLS UP in his classic convertible Camaro with the top down and honks his horn. I walk out to him sitting there with his Seals cap on backwards, grinning from ear to ear. His stereo blaring, "It's a Long Way to the Top," by AC/DC.

"I take it you had a good morning?" I ask and shake my head.

"Is it that obvious?" He chuckles.

"How many more days of super happy Martin should I be expecting?"

"Are you complaining? It doesn't impact my playing. I'm not like Seno who gets all emo when he doesn't have his woman with him."

"Not complaining," I smile.

"Actually, I bet I hit better when she's here."

"I'll take that action. Hitting challenge in the cave for batting practice?"

He nods and pulls into his parking spot in the player's garage.

"SINCE YOU THINK you're better when the woman is around, you go first," I say to Martin and gesture toward the batting cage.

He puts his helmet on and swings his bat around before grabbing sandpaper to do some quick work on it. He stretches from side to side and steps into the cage. He presses the button to start the pitches and stands ready. Pitch after pitch he smashes the ball, home run after home run. He steps out of the cage, "What did I tell you?"

I lean on my bat, "Try for some grounders."

He nods and a couple pitches in he's smacking grounders.

Martin steps out of the cage and nods at me, "Let's see what you've got."

I start with grounders and move to runs, not missing any pitches and smashing just as many as he did. "So, with your logic I'll hit even better when I have a woman?"

"Yes. Especially if she's at the game."

"Adding that she needs to like baseball to my list," I grin.

CHAPTER SIXTEEN

Maggie

Batting practice is on my mind again. If I'm not at batting practice how can he decide to walk up to me at the net and kiss me? I have to put myself in the position for it to happen or there's no chance that it will. As it is, the chance of Drew Brandt deciding to notice me is small and the chance he comes to me and kisses me? Even smaller. Both depressingly low statistical odds. Not as low as a woman he's never met or a woman who doesn't work at the stadium or a woman who lives on the other side of the country or a woman that's never heard of baseball, so I guess there's that. If I don't put myself in his path, it's going to stay that way. However, I can increase my odds by placing myself in his immediate zone. He's, statistically speaking, more likely to meet a woman and talk to her if she's repeatedly within a 20-foot radius than say a 40-foot or 60-foot radius. Purely the impact of location makes the odds better. Though, the bus shelter is approximately 85 feet from his house and hiding there with my NVGs isn't going to increase my odds with him and in many ways it could cause elimination of being a possibility all together. Such as when he has me arrested and presses charges against me for being a stalker, then there'll probably be a restraining order against me and I won't be allowed within 100 feet of him. Interesting, the punishment of increasing the distance between us by 15 feet. I bet I could still get a decent view with my goggles.

What am I thinking?

I get ready and go to the stadium early to watch batting practice from the safety of the press box.

The game starts slow, but in the 4th inning Seno slams it out of the park with the bases loaded. Seno excels with players on base, hitting a double or a home run 71% of the time. On the flip side of that, he's average with nobody on unless it means losing the game.

Overall a quiet game with no reply from the visiting team. Seals win 4-0.

The team has been playing at a high level and consistently getting better according to the stats. The players have said this team plays to win all season. As a lifelong Seals fan, it excites me and I'm hoping to be here for a world series run.

On my walk home I take the short route and walk right past his house on the sidewalk in front of it. The lights are already on again. I walk to the end of the street, cross the street and walk back to the other corner to get a good angle of all the lit windows and consider other locations to make camp in. I end up back at the bus shelter because it gives me the best view of his shower.

What am I doing? I don't have bail money. This can't end well. Why would he be interested in a woman who is, well, for lack of a word with positive connotation, stalking him? The subject of my surveillance mode course sounds so much better. Why did he have to move into my neighborhood anyway? It makes this all his fault. I'm supposed to simply ignore the high-profile professional athlete that lives a couple streets over from me? Moreover, somebody needs to be watching out for him. You never know when there could be a real threat to his safety. I'm playing the part of security watchman. If only I hadn't been in love with him since I was 12. Woah! Is that a valid statement? Am I in love with him? If it is, then theoretically my plea could be momentary lapse of judgement due to emotional insanity. Logically, I can't be in love with him until the chemistry between us has been confirmed. How does that impact the values and results for the matchmaking algorithm? I start a note on my phone titled matchmaking and add things to consider. Maybe I'm in lust? Amazing how just thinking the word sets, "Lust to Love," by the Go-Go's off playing in my head. Why am I doing this?

Just then the lights downstairs go off and he's standing in front of his open bedroom window pulling his shirt off over his head. My brain finally stops rambling and I silently enjoy the view. He grasps his windowsill with both hands and leans his head outside with his eyes closed. I can only imagine that he's enjoying the cool breeze on his face or possibly inhaling the warm scent of the jasmine trees lining the parkway. He backs away from his window and closes it, disappearing from view again.

"How long are you going to stand there and wait for him to show up again?" Caroline says quietly in my ear.

I jump out of my skin, "Don't do that!"

"Me?" Caroline questions.

"Yes you! Do you see anybody else here walking up behind me like a ninja and scaring the crap out me?" My hand is over my heart trying to calm down.

"I'm not the one out here in the dark of night learning

surveillance mode on night vision goggles," she says and mimics air quotes. She shifts her stance, "Who lives there?"

"What are you talking about?"

"Enough of the evasive responses. Who?"

"There he is! He's in the shower again," I focus on Drew and ignore my roommate.

"Aren't you at least going to let me see?"

"He's washing his hair. Oh...."

"What?"

"He's stroking his cock."

"How can you tell? Wait! Are you trying to suck me into your antics?"

"I'm just giving you the play by play. He's so sexy standing in the shower. His cock must be huge for me to catch glimpses of his tip with the height of that window."

"So, you've been out here watching whoever this guy is whack off?"

"No, this is the first time he's done that. And he's not *whoever*. That's Drew Brandt."

"The baseball player?"

"Yes."

"Isn't he the one you've had a crush on for like ever?"

"It's not a crush. We belong together."

"Stalker."

"He's the one who moved into my neighborhood."

"You're the one who bought tactical grade night vision goggles," she glares at me.

"That's not my fault either. The pawn shop guy suggested they'd do a better job than binoculars at night."

"Did he also give you books on surveillance and stalking?"

"You're going to get me noticed. SSSsshhhhh!"

"How am I the problem here?"

"Damn it!"

"What?"

"His lights all went off when I was being distracted by you." I take off my goggles and pack them into my backpack. "Let's go home."

"This is really what you've been doing the last few nights?"

"Yep."

"You weren't avoiding me. Good. But you're stalking a professional baseball player and that's definitely bad."

"I understand that. So, why am I doing it anyway?"

"Are you asking me or was that rhetorical?"

"If you have an answer I'll take it, otherwise consider it rhetorical."

"Infatuation."

"I'm not a boy-crazy teenager. I'm a scientist. There must be a logical explanation." I stop mid-step on our walk home and turn to face Caroline, "I have a business idea and I think we should go into business together."

"Okay, what is it?"

"Matchmaking service. We can get started on it after you get your coffee shop franchised and I get my masters completed. It will have an online presence and an app. I've already got notes for the algorithm and thoughts about assigning variables to each aspect of the candidates' personality and the factors of love."

Caroline stands there staring at me blankly.

I stare right back at her waiting for her response.

"Are you serious?"

"Yes."

"You think you can numerate human emotions?"

I shrug my shoulders, "Everything has a value."

"Have you considered the value assigned to the bail bond I'm going to have to pay when you get arrested?"

"You haven't told me what the logical explanation is yet."

"You're all over the place," she shakes her head and walks toward home.

"Are you going to help me or not?"

"If we have to move because we live within the distance of the restraining order I'm going to be pissed."

"That's not funny!"

CHAPTER SEVENTEEN

Drew

Typically I'm asleep as soon as my head hits the pillow. I've always been a hot shower before bed kind of guy. It relaxes me, kind of washes the day away so I can go to bed fresh and wake up with a clean slate. Tonight, I can't get comfortable. My brain is running on overdrive. I keep hearing Martin and Carter tell me I'm after someone from my past and how to find her, or my mom suggesting someone. Maybe it's just this house. Visiting my grandparents here as a child it was always a safe, warm place filled with love and family. It still has the same vibe, but there's nobody here with me. There's no kids running around, and nobody in the kitchen or entertaining. Everything is perfect, clean, and exactly how the designer left it. I love it, but it's missing the lived-in imperfections and family touches. The marks on the wall showing how children are growing taller. The homemade art that means more than keeping stylistic design intact. Mostly, it's quiet. Too quiet and me rattling around in this big house alone makes it worse. Thing is, that doesn't mean I want or need a woman. Maybe I need a roommate or a pet or both because I'm gone too much to have a pet and keep it alive. I'm an adult man and it doesn't seem right to have a roommate, it'd be different if I needed help with the rent or something but that's not the case. Women? I do have a desire for companionship. Someone to spend time with, share things with, relax with. I can't go for a walk around the stadium, pick a woman out of her seat, and claim her as the one. It's simply not how things work. I guess I've always assumed the right woman would somehow show up and I'd just know it was her, done. The older I get the more I question the theory. Seeing how happy Martin's woman makes him and how she impacts his game makes me want it more. How do I find a woman who will make me happy like that? Do I wait for her to find me? Will she show up in front of me someplace unexpected? Mostly, how important is it that she's from my past? Talk about limiting my options, that turns the sea of fish into an extra small kiddie pool.

I roll over frustrated and rearrange my pillows for the fifth time. I straighten my blanket and loosen the tuck on the top sheet. Nothing's helping. Finally, I close the automatic blackout blinds in my room and the pitch-black wins me some sleep.

I WAKE up earlier than normal and get up. I go for a walk around my neighborhood and find a coffee stand that smells like heaven. It's a quirky place with a barista dressed like she's starring in a workout video from the 1980's. I walk up to order and the barista about falls backwards, "Are you okay?"

"Yes, of course. A little case of de ja vu is all," she replies. "What can I get for you?"

"Coffee."

"Would you like to try one of our healthier drinks? A fresh juice or smoothie maybe?"

"I need coffee."

"You can get both. You only live once," she smiles up at me.

"What do you suggest?"

"Well, I've been told I make the best coffee anywhere, but I think you should try my special smoothie too. Supplement the coffee with some vitamins."

"I'll leave it to you then," I smile.

"Here's your coffee, go ahead and pay on the notepad right there," she points to the digital notepad on the counter and I take the coffee in my hand inhaling the enticing aroma. "I'll have your smoothie ready in a few minutes."

I lean against the stand drinking my coffee and watching as other customers place orders and pick-up to-gos. An adorably tired looking woman walks up wearing an oversized sweatshirt and without saying a word gets handed a cup of coffee, and turns around disappearing to wherever she came from. Odd. Why is she familiar? Warm and cozy in her Seals hoodie.

"Here's your smoothie, sir," the barista calls out and waves at me.

I pick a purple drink up off the counter, "What is it?"

She smiles, "Try it and tell me if you like it first."

I nod and go along with her. I take a sip and it's almost as good as the coffee but with a frosty smooth mouth feel, "Tasty. I like the texture."

"Pomegranate Power," she points to it on the menu board revealing the multitude of vegetables and greens in it on top of the pomegranate and açaí. "You can always use more power, right?" She winks at me and obviously knows who I am.

"It can't hurt," I smile back. "How do I get on the walk up and you hand me my coffee program?"

"If I know your order I'll make it when I see you coming."

"Is the oversized hoodie and silence required?" I chuckle.

"Oh! That's my roommate. She's not human until she has her coffee."

"Thank you. I'll be back again soon." I drop a $10 bill in her tip jar and take the last drink of my coffee before I continue my walk.

The neighborhood is different in the morning. Fresh, bright, and busy with people going through their daily routine. Or, in the case of the adorable oversized hoodie girl, simply trying to get some coffee in their system so they can get their day started. I walk around surveying the neighborhood interested to see what the other homeowners have done to preserve the historical buildings, until my phone starts buzzing.

Martin: Do we have a workout plan today?
Me: I'm just waiting on you.
Me: Up for the stadium run?
Martin: I'm ready for anything. I'll pick you up.
Me: Okay.

I walk home and Martin is already there waiting for me, I hop into his car.

CHAPTER EIGHTEEN

Maggie

"Mags!" Caroline yells for me when she comes through the door. "Maggie!"

"I'm in my room," I yell back.

She's instantly in my doorway and out of breath, her hands grasping the doorframe around her.

"What's wrong? Are you okay?" I ask concerned.

"I ran home," her breathing heavy.

"Why would you do that? Run," I glare at her thinking she's lost her sanity.

"It's your fault."

"Just like everything else, but why this time?"

"I wanted to get home as quick as I could to tell you what happened."

I stare at her waiting for the information that made her *run*. I wait. "Are you going to tell me?"

"Oh, yes. It was him. The baseball player guy that was whacking off in the shower."

She has my attention, "You saw Drew?"

"Yes. That's what I just told you."

"Where did you see Drew?"

"He stopped by the stand and ordered coffee. And he let me upsell him a smoothie."

"What did you do?"

Caroline glares at me like it should be obvious, "I made him a house coffee and a pomegranate power smoothie."

"I get it. His eyes are as clear and beautiful as the ocean at a tropical beach. He was friendly and left me a $10 tip," her eyes shining.

"You get what?"

"Your utter infatuation with the man."

"You talked to him?"

"Oh, yeah! That's what I wanted to tell you," she stops and changes her train of thought again. "He was there when you picked up your coffee. Does that tell you how dependent you are on caffeine? You walked right by your dream man, got your coffee, turned around and went home without noticing."

"Ugh!" How is that possible?

"But..." She holds her finger up at me.

"But what?" I wish she would get on with it already.

"Hold on, this is the part I ran home for." Caroline straightens, "He asked me how to get the pick-up service like the adorable girl in the oversized hoodie."

"He liked my hoodie?"

"Listen... he said *adorable girl* in the oversized hoodie."

"He didn't say that. I'm sure you misheard him or got the words mixed up since he said them. Are you sure it was even him?"

"It was him and I know exactly what he said! Why wouldn't he say that? Other than you did have a bit of your grumpy face on, but I get where some could find that charming," Caroline quirks her head to the side.

"What do you mean I had my grumpy face on?" I question.

"You know when you aren't actually awake but you're out of bed and moving, kind of zombie-like? You don't speak and if you make any noise at all it's more of a grunt. You were completely silent today, so don't worry about that part."

"I don't do that," I state clearly.

"Yeah, you do. You even had your hood up this morning and hadn't brushed your hair yet. Now that I think about it, you might've been wearing your pajama pants."

"Your coffee was amazing this morning. Thank you."

"You're welcome. Anyway, he said he'd be back. And I don't care what you think, he thinks you're adorable."

"Did you say anything about me?"

"I told him you're my roommate and don't function until you've had your coffee. Nothing heinous."

"Anything else?"

"He asked for your name and address so he could file a restraining order against you." Caroline smiles, "Just kidding."

I immediately make a change in my plans for the day. "I've gotta go. I'm going to watch batting practice today."

"Go girl!" Caroline claps with glee.

I get ready to go and fight with myself. Should I wear the huge oversized hoodie from this morning so he recognizes me or something different so it wasn't obviously me out getting coffee in my pajamas? I shove the hoodie in my backpack, change into my Seals shirt, fix my hair, and walk out the door.

Walking to the stadium I wonder if it's possible that Caroline got it right. Did he say I'm adorable? I don't think anyone has said I'm adorable since I was 3 years old. I've been told I'm annoying. I've been told to stop with the numbers, apparently everyone doesn't believe in science. My mom likes to tell me that I should dress more like a female. The guy that took me to the prom told me I was beautiful, but I'm pretty sure he needed glasses. He kept squinting his eyes and puckering his lips, it was weird.

I go through the employee security gate and up to the press box to leave my backpack under my desk. The score-keeper is already at his desk, "You're early."

"I want to sit down by the field and watch batting practice," I reply.

"You usually watch batting practice from here. Doesn't matter, coach held batting practice early today."

"Of course he did." Just my luck. I finally get the sign I've been waiting for and the opportunity is taken away. I dig my current read out of my backpack and kick back in my chair until game time.

CHAPTER NINETEEN

Drew

The team is all in the locker room having a good time and everything is off kilter for me. I appreciate a consistent routine and coach held batting practice early. It happens. Too much free time turns into music blaring, some of the guys playing video games, and a full table playing poker. I relax on the sofa and rest my eyes, trying to make up for the sleep I lost last night. I need to be ready for the game.

MARTIN WAKES me from a dead sleep, "Time to wake up sleeping beauty!"

I sit up and stretch, much more rested than I was before. How I managed to sleep I have no idea, but I must've needed it.

"Let's get out early and warm up. You can tell me all about Becky," Martin says waggling his eyebrows.

"Who's Becky?" I ask confused.

"Bro, you were talking in your sleep."

"Crap."

"Don't worry. You kept saying "no mom" and "not Becky," nothing else."

We get out of the locker room and Martin continues, "So, spill. Who's Becky?"

"I don't know anyone named Becky."

"You told your mom no repeatedly and kept saying not Becky. It must be something."

It hits me, "My mom offered to set me up with her friend's daughter, Becky."

Martin nods, "This wanting a chick thing has you in knots, doesn't it?"

"I had a hard time falling asleep last night. My brain wouldn't turn off. It's all I could think about. I'll get it figured out." We warm up throwing the ball back and forth silently as the stadium fills with fans.

The game has always been natural for me. Playing is a reaction, like a knee jerk—no thought required. It's part of me. The more I do it, the better my reactions get. Other parts of my life are different. Logical, common sense things are a no-brainer, but everything else makes me stop and think. Martin is 100% right when he says I'm an over-thinker. I search for the reasoning in everything. I want to understand why so I can make the best decision every time. The problem is life doesn't work like that. For now, I'm going to let all of this go and become the game.

It's been one of those small ball games. Which is great when I'm running the base paths and a grind on defense. I took a beating on the defensive side of things today, dirty and bruised up from diving for it. While the adrenaline rush from stealing bases makes me want to do it again. I'm number two on the team to Cross in successful stolen bases, he's slightly faster than me and willing to take more risks on the base paths—rightfully so with his record. I don't want to make a stupid out and hurt the team. I'm skilled with my bat and not afraid to hit one down the line and run it out or bloop it over a baseman. There's something to be said for grounders, I don't always have to go for it. There's strategy involved in this game and swinging for the fence every time doesn't get us where we want to be. We have a goal and that's to win—the game, the series, the championship. It seems a bit arrogant, but we've adopted the stance as a team and there's no going back.

It was in the 12th inning when we lost it. You get that far into extra innings and it's really a competition of which team will screw up first. We're all tired though we try not to show it. It was a battle. Every time we scored they scored. I'm happy it's over. Seals lost 15-14.

After trouble sleeping last night and the long game, I can't wait to get home. On the walk home my brain clicks back over and won't shut off. I walk through my door and directly to the kitchen wondering if my mom thought to stock my panty or refrigerator with any alcohol. My refrigerator is stocked with a mixed 6-pack of beer, a bottle of champagne, and a bottle of Moscato. My pantry has fifths of Jack, Jose, and Stoli, as well as a couple bottles of red wine. I know better than to drink too much during the season, but I've got to shut my mind off. Jose has my attention. I don't bother with a shot glass and take two shots straight from the bottle. I lock up the bottom half of the house and get the lights turned off before I go upstairs taking the bottle with me. My master suite is huge, bigger than my old apartment. I've got a king-sized four poster bed with a matching solid oak dresser, night stands, armoire and standing mirror, as well as a recliner and loveseat all in my bedroom. I have a huge TV mounted on the wall in the corner. My walk-in closet is as big as some bedrooms and has a bench in the middle of it as well as a suit butler. I've got a cabinet in the back of the closet with all of my trophies and awards for sports in it. I take another slug from the bottle of tequila. The designer decorated my master suite in burgundy with assorted textures, accented with cream and navy. She calls it a masculine take on historical red, white, and blue. It's mostly burgundy and it's grown on me, especially the textures like the velvet bed set with the jersey knit sheets. It's cozy and comforting. The walls are the cream color and the wall with windows has drapes all the way across it made of a burgundy corduroy. Everything comes together to give the room some weight and an inviting masculine feel.

I take another drink and all I want to do is let go. I open my window and the cool night air blows against my face. A breeze blows the draperies around me. I stand with my hands on the window sill, still learning my surroundings and notice a bright green light moving around in the bus shelter at the corner. How odd. Maybe someone waiting for the bus has their phone charger out or something. I wait and watch. The green light moves and stops, sitting on top of the fence next to the bus shelter. I try to focus. I turn the lights off in my room and check again. Is someone watching me? I close the window and move to my bathroom. I turn my shower on and open the window, if they want to watch me then I'm going to give them a show. I take another drink. Fuck I need to get laid. That's probably my whole problem. I handled it myself last night and I'll do it again tonight. I strip naked and step into my shower, leaning out the window showing my bare torso to the world but specifically whoever it is who's watching me. I scrub my hand over my face and slide it down my chest, across my abs until I can grasp my cock. My hard cock needs some attention. I give it one long good stroke while I stare directly at the green light. I lean my head back and stroke it again, tugging on it hard. I check to make sure the person is still watching and smile, as I close my eyes and continue to pleasure myself. I'm so fucking hard and need to release. I gaze down toward the green light and crook my finger toward them, gesturing for them to come over. Within seconds the light is gone, but they aren't walking toward my door. The oversized hoodie from this morning is walking off in the opposite direction.

Could the adorable girl in the oversized hoodie be stalking me?

I satisfy myself, since nobody else is going to do it, take another shot, and go to bed. Out before I could close the window.

CHAPTER TWENTY

Maggie

"Caroline!" I scream as I try to get the door unlocked.

She opens the door, "What's wrong?"

I get into our apartment quickly, lock the door securely, and turn off all the lights.

"Ummm. What are you doing?" Caroline asks me.

"SSshhhhh."

"Okay, what are you doing?" She asks much quieter.

"He saw me and I don't know if he knows it was me or not and he was whacking off again but it was like he was whacking it for my benefit. I swear he invited me over while he was hanging out the window of his shower with his cock in his hand!"

"Hold on! First, are you sure? How much caffeine have you had today? How could he even see you? You should have mad surveillance skills by now."

"It's not funny! What if he's following me and on his way here right now?"

"Does this mean you're going to stop with the night vision goggles?"

"I'm definitely not doing it tomorrow night."

"Good. Commit to one day at a time."

"Well, why would I tomorrow when the team is away? He won't be home."

On a deep sigh, "It's a start and the road trip gives you some time to consider what you're doing and what might happen since you've been caught."

"I don't know that he knows it's me or that he knows who I am. It's all an unknown. Obviously I overreacted because he's not banging on our door right now."

"Do you realize you're wearing the oversized hoodie from this morning?"

"Fuck me."

"Sounds like he wanted to."

"Caroline!"

"You've been trying to get him to talk to you for what? 14 years? He finally invites you in and you run away."

"He still doesn't know who I am."

"He knows you're my roommate."

"You're going to have to deliver my coffee to me from now on."

"I will not!"

"What else am I supposed to do?"

"Keep doing what you've always done, or do what everybody else does and make your own at home."

"That's not fair. This is for both of us. You already said you don't want to move because of the restraining order. When he figures out who I am that's the first thing he'll do."

"I'm sorry, which one of us is having sex with Drew Brandt?"

"AAhhh! I'm not having sex with anyone."

"That's your own fault."

"Of course back to everything is my fault." I throw my hands in the air.

"Not everything, but if it was me I'd be at his place right now and not having this conversation. And, I haven't been crushing on him for half my life."

"Are you telling me to go over there now?"

"No. It's too late. He's already whacked off and gone to bed by now. You'd just be waking him up," Caroline shakes her head. "Plus, you probably don't want to start something the night before he leaves for a road trip."

"Start something? You think running to his front door when he wants sex is starting something?"

"What else do you think you're going to get when you're his stalker? It's not like you're his friend or his love interest," Caroline throws her hands in the air.

"Didn't he say I'm adorable?" I shoot back rhetorically.

"I could be a possible love interest," I say in a sweet voice.

"You could also be an entertaining zombie. Possibly a sex slave." She cocks her head to the side, "If you're not interested in the sex slave position let me know, I'd do it," she says decisively.

"Caroline!" I shout in shock.

"What? He's hot. He's conveniently located. He's got gorgeous eyes. And, according to you, he's got a huge cock. What's not to like? I'm in," she smiles.

I glare at her wondering if I've got competition in the Drew Brandt race.

"Don't worry. I wouldn't touch him with a ten-foot pole unless you gave me permission first. But, if you give me permission? Game on! Who doesn't want a ballplayer of their very own?"

"He's more than that. I'd want him even if he didn't play. He's sweet, ethical, and smart."

"Don't forget horny. He's definitely horny."

"That just proves he's not with anybody else," I add to the conversation.

"Good point. But he could've been inviting any standard bus rider up. There's no way he could see you."

"I'm wearing the hoodie, he may have recognized it."

"Does that make you the adorable stalker in the oversized hoodie?" She laughs.

CHAPTER TWENTY-ONE

Drew

It's a team travel day. I pull my pickup out of the garage and toss my luggage in the back. I secure my house and set the alarm.

Me: Road trip starts today. Alarm is set at the house.
Mom: Thank you for letting me know. Have a safe trip honey.

I drive the few blocks to the stadium and pull into the player's garage. I park and unload, leaving my suitcase with the others to get checked and keeping my backpack with me.

Martin pulls into the garage and calls out to me, "Wait for me!"

I nod in reply. This morning has been all business, getting packed and ready for the road trip. I slept like a baby and I'm hoping to sleep more on the plane. I remember last night slowly. There was half a fifth sitting on my nightstand when I woke up this morning. I didn't think I drank that much, but I can't argue with the evidence. The adorable girl in the oversized hoodie was watching me. A grin spreads across my face at the thought.

"What are you all smiley about?" Martin chuckles.

"I might have a stalker," I say on a laugh.

"That's nothing to laugh about. Stalkers are dangerous. Serious trouble," he shakes his head.

"I'm not worried about this one. She took off when I caught her watching me, but I'm pretty sure I saw her at the coffee stand yesterday."

"Stop right there. Stalkers are bad."

I shrug, "Maybe."

"Dude, you're asking for trouble."

I laugh, "I kind of did last night."

"What did you do?"

"I stood naked in my window and gestured to her to come over."

"You're crazy," Martin shakes his head.

"Blame the tequila."

I sit next to Martin on the flight and he won't let the stalker thing go. "Seriously, I'm not worried about it."

"A stalker is a stalker." He stands up, "Who has had a stalker?" A few of the guys lift a hand and the comments start flying around the plane. "Okay, Brandt may have a stalker and he's not taking it seriously. Anybody want to join us and explain to him it's not a joking matter? It's a three-hour flight and we have plenty of time." He sits back down and grins at me.

"Why'd you do that?"

"You need to know."

"I want to sleep."

"You can sleep later."

Lucky Lucine takes the seat next to us and quietly clears his throat, "You can never know with women. Sometimes they seem normal and you take them on one date, but you decide they aren't for you. Next thing you know you've got a stalker waiting and watching for you to leave the house so they can follow you and find out if you're dating anyone else and then harass whoever you're dating. Even worse, two women you date only once become friends," he nods and opens his eyes wide. "Need I say more?" His whole body shivers, "I can't even talk about it." He gets up and leaves quickly.

Pitcher Tommy Knight calmly sits with us, never turning to make eye contact, "You never know where they will show up. You come out of the grocery store and find them sitting in your car, sometimes naked. Passed out in front of your apartment door with a note addressed to you in their hand, and all you want to do is get inside but you can't because if you push the door open they will fall into your apartment. I don't want her in my apartment for any reason. I went to the hotel instead and called the police to deal with getting her moved. Then on road trips you think you're finally rid of her, but she's there too. She talks her way into your hotel room, saying she's your woman. She picks up your food order and plays the part of delivery person. I never spoke to her, not once. I just wanted her to go away." He left suddenly, not wanting to talk about it.

Mark Rock saunters down the aisle, passes us and then comes back to join us. "Hey, you having stalker trouble?"

"Not really," I reply.

Martin sighs, "He doesn't get it. It makes him happy that the chick likes him."

"She was persistent. Not bad to look at. Gave me head whenever I wanted. She didn't leave even when I ignored her. But she also didn't annoy me. I should never have opened the door the night she whispered through my hotel room door at me telling me all the things she wanted to do to my cock—it was an around the world scenario starting with swallowing my cock and ending with banging her backdoor. She became my pleasure whenever I wanted and whatever I wanted. So, rather than figuring out how to get rid of her I married her. She disappeared a week later and I've never seen her again. I had the marriage annulled. Still can't find head that compares. Tortures me to this day." Rock gazes at the floor and shakes his head as he gets up and leaves.

After a few minutes our closer Doug Houck sits down, but doesn't say anything.

"Does this have anything to do with why everybody calls you Super D?" Martin asks.

Doug grins, "No. Nothing about that has to do with my stalkers. I couldn't have the woman I wanted. I settled for women I thought liked me, not seeing the warning signs. You know the ones, the player-chasing gold diggers. I'd take them to dinner a couple times and then back to my place for sex. There were a few of them at the same time, a couple in other places to keep me happy on road trips. I never once made a commitment, but after half a dozen dates and incomparable orgasms—they assumed. I'm not an ass, I took mine but I always gave them theirs. Then they'd go all Fatal Attraction on me when they saw me with somebody else. That's not my life anymore. I got the one I wanted. It's so much better. Communication is key even if the chick doesn't matter, set

93

expectations." He takes a deep breath and goes back to his seat.

Seno slides in next to us after the others have all gone back to their seats, "I've never had a stalker that I'm aware of. I know one thing for sure, you have to be you and do what you want. One guy's stalker could be another's perfect match. At least you know she likes you." He raises his eyebrows and smiles, going back to his seat without another word.

I chuckle, "What did we learn here today?"

"I don't know man, some of our teammates are fucked up." We both laugh quietly and I finally get some sleep.

CHAPTER TWENTY-TWO

Maggie

The team is gone and I've decided it's a good thing. It allows me time to make a plan and prepare. First, I'm definitely going to start attending batting practice and sitting down by the field. Second, I need to get a thermos to send to work with Caroline so she can bring me coffee back for the next morning and I can avoid the coffee stand. Third, well I'm torn. Do I continue to hang out in the bus shelter, or somewhere else with a good vantage point, with my goggles watching for activity, or sell my NVGs back to the pawn shop? It's not worth selling them back, I'd be lucky to get $60. I may be able to use them for something else in the future, you never know when a neighborhood battle might break out and the electricity might be out—the goggles could come in handy. Maybe during an eclipse. If I continue my surveillance course, ahem, I need to start looking for a new place to live and be prepared to move. I don't want to move. I want him. If I have to move I don't get him either. Fuck.

How can I be with him? What a question to ask about a man that doesn't know I exist. I may have to leave it up to batting practice. Or, maybe run into him walking home and start up a conversation? Am I going about this all wrong? I could run into him at the coffee stand, but then I have to be awake, functioning, and looking like a human before I leave the house and before I have the elixir that is my life's existence. Make coffee at home and then go have another cup? It doesn't leave much of a window for running into him unless I hang out at the coffee stand and why would I be doing that? They don't even have a table or chair. It's not like those coffee places with the free Wi-Fi that everyone congregates at, and that doesn't matter because Caroline truly makes the best coffee. I suppose I could have coffee and stand around harassing Caroline while I drink it, and then have a smoothie if I need to stretch the time a bit. It would make her happy if I drank a smoothie. No need to alter the space-time continuum.

I add new information to my thesis, reviewing the numbers and considering the chart trajectories. I've been using Seno, Brandt, and Cross as sample subjects for comparisons, but I'm seeing a correlation between Seno and Cross, so I added Martin as a sample subject. I'm wondering if there's measurable value in players pairing up together. The numbers suggest it's a possibility. I search for players that have teamed up on other teams and in the past, and gather their stats to compare pre and post pairing. The follow up question being: Is player value impacted when the player he's paired with gets traded? Interesting things that will support my thesis.

I spend days on autopilot, searching for paired players and their stats, walking over to get my coffee, watching the game and keeping score while focused on the connection between the different players, and making notes every postgame. Caroline has been trading off with me on food duties since we're both focused on goals. The team will be back soon. Hopefully, I'll have this part of my thesis complete by then.

I stop and take the time to go through my email, I've been so absorbed with my thesis I've neglected it for a few days. Multiple emails from the university. I need to check in with my advisor this week. And this is different, an invite to the annual Researching the Sciences Banquet including my ticket. Usually I have to buy a ticket and talk myself out of going because I don't want to spend the money, though it's all a donation to the science department. I read further... "Caroline!" I run to find her.

"Yea? I'm in the kitchen."

I find her baking her special biscuits, measuring with scientific precision and making notes as she goes. "I got an invite to the annual banquet and I'm one of the honorees!"

She turns to me, "Good job!" She high fives me. "That means you have to go this year."

"Yea. What do I wear?"

"When is it?"

"Next weekend."

"We have time to figure that out after my biscuits are baked," she says bending over to level off a cup of flour before she weighs it. "Is it business casual, semi-formal, formal?"

I read for more details, "It's evening cocktail attire."

She stops and glares at me, "Do you have any high heels?"

"Yes."

"Get them out and bring them to me, please."

"It can wait until after the biscuits."

"Now, please."

"Yes, ma'am." I go to my closet and pull the box of dress shoes down from the top shelf. I take it back to the kitchen with me and take the lid off to show Caroline what I've got.

"The ballet flats are not an option. Those brown ones look like they belonged to your grandmother. Do you have anything that's from this century?"

"This is what I have," I huff.

"I'd let you borrow mine but we don't wear the same size. We have shoe shopping in our future, and not at the pawn shop."

"But they're cheaper at the pawn shop."

"They're old and disgusting, or super expensive name brands at the pawn shop."

"Fine. When and where?"

"We can go when I'm done with the biscuits."

"I can't there's a game."

"I'll pre-shop online while you keep score."

"What about the dress?"

"You don't want to wear a circa 1970's pantsuit?"

"I can't fake this, I'm being honored. I'll probably have to walk up to the stage and say thank you or something."

"That's why we're starting with the shoes. You're going to spend every minute you are home in those shoes to get comfortable in them and skilled at walking in them. I don't want the shoes to be an extra obstacle on an evening that's probably already going to be uncomfortable."

"This is why I asked you."

"You came to the right person," she says with confidence. "Any idea what kind of dress?"

"Not long, but not short. Fancy, but respectable. Definitely a dark color."

"Can I take advantage of this opportunity to show off your figure?"

"I suppose."

"Yay!" She claps and flour puffs off her hands.

CHAPTER TWENTY-THREE

Drew

One thing about long road trips, they get me out of my head. Clear the slate. After days in Texas, Ohio, and Missouri, I'm ready to go home. It's fun to get out with the team and hit the bar, but I'm ready for some quiet and a home-cooked meal.

As far as the games, they've gone well. I'm not saying any more than that because I'm not going to be the one to jinx it.

We came home to a series against Washington.

I'm wondering if my stalker will be back. I considered leaving her an invite in the bus shelter, but thought better of it because I can't control who will find it. I've considered Martin's point and maybe stalker isn't the right word for her, but I don't have a clue what else to call someone who's been observing me with NVGs. Maybe a voyeur though she wouldn't have expected me to strip for her. Man, I want to strip for her and get that oversized hoodie off of her. It was obvious she has an attractive feminine shape to her, the way her clothes hung on her. But that hoodie? We could both fit in there together, and now that's on my bucket list. I'm getting in that hoodie with her.

On the other side of things, Seno may have the right idea. One man's stalker could be another man's wife. Or in the case of Rock, you could marry your stalker. I really do have some teammates with fucked up history, and the worst part of it was witnessing how hard it was for them to talk about it, how affected they are by it. Part of it is that they make bad choices. Who would marry their stalker? Then again, I want to date mine.

CHAPTER TWENTY-FOUR

Maggie

I wake up to knocking on my bedroom door, "What?"

"Good morning to you, too," my roommate replies as she opens my door. "I'm expecting a few orders to get delivered today while I'm at work. Can you keep an eye out and bring them in for me?"

I rustle under the blankets, not ready to be awake, "No problem. Can I sleep another hour first?"

"That should be fine. I doubt any of them get delivered before 11am."

"But, it's..." I check my phone, "5:30am." I roll over and pull the blankets up over my head.

"Yeah, some of us get up and go to work at this time every morning. Thanks!"

I don't make another sound and she leaves, closing my door behind her. I rearrange the blankets and snuggle in with the blankets around my neck. There's a squeal and I sit up straight and throw the blankets back searching for Frank to find him wrapped up in the edge of the blanket I had snuggled into. I pull him out and place him gently on my pillow, "Sorry Frank, you're safer on my pillow." He clicks a few times and nuzzles into my hair as both of us fall back to sleep.

WHEN I FINALLY GET UP, dressed, and ready to go get my coffee there's a barricade of packages at the door blocking me from leaving. I take all the packages in, making a pile on the coffee table. Packages of varying sizes and weights. Some boxes and some bags.

Once the way has been cleared I lock the door behind me and make my way over to the coffee stand. It's a warm morning and the sun is making everything shine. I walk up to the coffee stand and Caroline nods at me, "How many packages are you expecting today?"

"I'm not sure. I didn't count them. Did any get delivered?"

"Eleven so far."

"Huh, okay. There's probably a few more."

She hands me my coffee and for a moment the world is a beautiful place, nobody could ruin my day if they tried. "Thank you." I lift my cup to her and turn around to walk home.

"Hey! Can you stop and pick up a couple things?"

Crap. "What?"

"Just walk into the drug store on the corner and grab some pasties and boob tape. Would be great. Thank you."

Double crap. Sometimes I wonder how much my free coffee actually costs me.

I get home to more boxes and bring them in. It's a day

game today because the team flies home tonight, so I settle in to watch the game and keep score.

The pregame show is all about Brandt and Martin. After the games yesterday finished their stats show them just shy of the top player duo, less than a half percent difference in all categories and number one in the most successful double plays. It's huge when you compare the numbers from last year and the beginning of the season. They interview Brandt:

Interviewer: Drew, what do you think has impacted your game numbers so much specifically over the last few weeks? It's truly amazing to see the growth. Is it all your kind of partnership with Martin or do you think there's anything else to it?

Drew: (nervous chuckle) Working out with Martin on a daily basis is huge for me, he helps to keep me grounded and pushes me to be better. Honestly, now that I live downtown I walk to and from the stadium most days, something about the walk home releases everything for me and helps me rest.

Interviewer: I love a walk around the neighborhood after work. It's refreshing. I have a little doggo I take out with me. How far is your walk?

Drew: I don't have a dog, it'd be too much for me with the grind of the season and I don't want to leave it with a sitter all the time. I'm going to plead the fifth on the last part of your question. I don't want to give everyone out there my address.

Interviewer: Well, thank you for taking the time to talk with me. Good luck today.

Drew: Thank you.

Good god he has gorgeous eyes, and that smile. His little chuckle is so sexy. I could listen to him all day with his deep articulate voice. Gah!

The game starts and I do my best to focus on keeping score and stats, but I'm distracted by the fact that he's coming home tonight. Focus on the game, not how hot his ass is in those pants! Don't get sucked into those clear blue lakes he has for eyes. It's his intensity that I cannot deny and I find myself admiring his attitude and drive on the field, simply the way he moves.

Caroline rattling the door pulls me from my trance. She pushes the door open and kicks more packages inside. "Hey," she says.

I raise my hand to her, "Still a few innings left."

"Okay, find me when you're done," she disappears into her bedroom, leaving me to the game.

CHAPTER TWENTY-FIVE

Drew

The team is tired. The relief pitchers need a break. We're all ready to go home and it was obvious in the way we played today. Corey Grace did his thing for the first seven innings, not a single hit. But the line of relief pitchers we ran out to the mound today got lit up, every single one of them. For me, the game was—let's just say I touched the ball once. No hits and home runs doesn't leave much for the second baseman to do. Not the way you want to end a road trip. I think we all need the off day tomorrow.

<hr>

I was asleep before the plane took off for home. All I want to do is climb into my own bed. We get back to the stadium and I go to the locker room to relax while they unload the luggage.

On my way Carter gets my attention, "Brandt, marketing

left some information on an event they want you to attend. I left it in your locker for you."

"Thank you," I did volunteer to attend events in the community for the team. I go to my locker and find the details.

> *Brandt,*
>
> *Thank you for helping to provide a face for the team in the community. We're hoping you're able to attend the Researching the Sciences Banquet at the university this weekend. There's no other player we'd love to have representing us more at this event, you're a perfect fit!*
>
> *The event is this Saturday at 7pm. A tuxedo would be appropriate attire. If you have questions or need help with transportation or attire, please let us know and we will be happy to assist. This is an event to raise money for the Science Departments and honor some of the studying scientists. The Seals have already made a generous donation, so please don't feel like you're required to do so.*
>
> *Please find your ticket to the event enclosed.*
>
> *Thank you,*
>
> *Marketing*

Any of my teammates would be complaining about getting this request after a road trip or any time really. I've been wondering if they forgot I volunteered. San Diego is home and I want to do my part to help and be part of the community. And the Researching the Sciences Banquet? Sounds like a real rager. I graduated from the university and spent some time in the Physics building, but nothing like the scientists who are being honored. They're dedicated and for me it was secondary to baseball.

CHAPTER TWENTY-SIX

Maggie

With the game finally over and no signs of Drew to distract me I find Caroline, "So should we go shopping?" I try to be chipper, but it doesn't sound fun to me—it sounds expensive.

Caroline gets a big grin on her face, "I already did." She gestures to all of the packages that have been delivered today, "It's time to play dress up Mags!" She grins from ear to ear, "I'll get everything open and ready, grab one of the bags and go put it on."

I stare at her, "This is all stuff for me to wear to the banquet?"

"It's choices. You don't worry about it. Try everything on and we'll choose a dress."

"There's so much."

"One at a time. I figure this is better than dragging you through the mall."

"Fair." I grab one of the bags and go to my room. I get it

open and pull out a fitted knee length black dress with spaghetti straps. It's a thick formal-looking brocade material and has a straight neckline. It zips up the back and I can't reach the zipper. "Caroline, help please," I say as I walk back to the living room. I stop in my tracks when I see the shoes all lined up on top of their boxes and dresses hanging in the doorway to her room. "You bought too much."

"I used my credit card and almost all of this will get returned, no big deal. Turn around."

I turn around obediently and she zips me up.

"That is fabulous on you, but I don't think it's the right vibe for your event. I forget you have such a slender figure, you've always got it hidden. What do you think? Can you see yourself wearing it?"

"I'm not this person. This doesn't go with my jeans and hoodie."

"You do sometimes have events and parties to attend."

"Yea."

"Every woman needs a black dress."

"I suppose. It's a little too sexy for the Science Departments."

"Fair enough." She unzips me and hands me the next dress to try on and shoos me back to my room.

I slither out of the black dress and stuff it back in its bag. The next one is a dark violet dress with cap sleeves and a sweetheart neckline. Not as fitted as the previous one, but belted at the waist. I walk out to Caroline, "This one's a no. Not my color at all and it makes me feel like an elementary school teacher." I toss the bag with the black dress in it to her.

"Fine. Here's the next one, go change." She nods.

I get out of the teacher costume and put it back on its hanger. The next dress is made of a linen charcoal grey material that's gathered at my waist in kind of a half-moon shape.

110

It has a professional style to it. I go show Caroline, "This one is fine, but kind of business casual to me. Nothing at all fancy or evening about it to me."

She nods, "I agree. It would be perfect for interviews or presenting your thesis."

"Possibly."

She hands me the next one, "I can't wait to see this one on you. It has more style to it and you'll probably hate it."

I roll my eyes at her and take it to my room. I hang the grey dress up in my doorway, maybe I should keep it. I'm going to need a dress for my thesis presentation and hopefully that happens in the next year. The next dress is navy blue with opulent beading on the upper part of the bodice, fitted down to my lower thigh and has a see-thru feminine skirt over the bottom half. It's fancy and flirty without being too sexy. "Caroline, what do you think of this one?" I ask as I walk out of my room. "I love the beading."

She claps, "Yes, that's the one!" She turns to the shoe line up and pushes the options that will go with the dress toward me. "Okay, they have to be at least somewhat comfortable and you have to be able to stand in them."

I step into the first pair. They're a basic navy satin heel and remind me of the pair I got dyed to match my prom dress, "I don't like the satin shoes with the dress material."

"Okay, next pair..." she says as she boxes up the shoes that I don't like.

I slide into high black heels with a peekaboo toe and a thin platform. Possibly too tall for me. I move my foot around in the shoe for Caroline to give me her opinion, "You're super tall and I don't think I like the black with the navy dress. How do they fit?"

"Pretty good, comfortable though I might get a nosebleed up here."

"I bet they'd look great with the grey dress," she gazes up at me.

I take them off and she boxes them up, setting them to the side with the grey dress. The next pair are shiny and match the beading on the dress. I try them on and I'm like Cinderella. "These ones."

"Hold on," Caroline says and checks me out. "You could also wear it to weddings, out to fine dining. It's a bit mature, but it does give the respectable air and the shoes make it with their peekaboo sparkle."

"How can it be mature when there's peekaboo sparkle?"

"I retract the mature comment. Peekaboo sparkle and beading for the win." She closes up the other shoes and gathers everything together, "I'm going to set up the returns on everything. I think you should keep the grey dress and black shoes."

"Not in my budget. I don't even know how much I'm spending on the navy dress and sparkle shoes."

"I'm sure neither of them cost as much as your night vision goggles," she smirks at me. "You can pay for one this month and the other next month."

"Okay. Thank you."

"Keep those shoes on and get some practice wearing them. You should wear your hair down and fluff it out a bit."

"I'll definitely wear it down." I stop when I remember, "The team is home tonight."

"Does that mean the goggles are going into use again?"

"I want to say no, but I'm still curious."

"It's a bad idea."

I walk into my room and check my goggles, they're out of charge. There you have it. The powers that be are saving me from myself. "I'm not using my goggles tonight."

She smiles, "Good."

"But I might go for a walk because I want to see if he got home."

"Mags, just let it be."

I nod and take my new dresses and shoes into my room.

Electronics should always be ready for action, so I plug my goggles in to charge.

I send an email to the scorekeeper requesting his book from the road trip, so I can compare and fill in any blanks I have.

I take the sparkly shoes off, slide into my sneakers, and pull my hoodie on. I call out to Caroline on my way out the door, "Want anything from the Creamery?"

She leans back and gazes at me from the kitchen with a worried expression, "Are you thinking cups, cones, or pints?"

"Whatever you want. The waffle cones are yummy, but they melt and get messy," I reply.

"It's not the only thing that could get messy. A single cup of Bourbon Butter Pecan would be delicious," she grins fully aware of what I'm doing.

"Don't look at me like that. Do you see my goggles or anywhere I could be hiding them?"

She stares at me, giving me the once over from my toes to the top of my head, "I don't see any goggles, but I know you."

I shake my head at her and walk out the door. The night air is cooler than it's been and it smells like rain. I pull my hood up over my head and shove my hands in my pocket. The Creamery is about seven blocks away and I choose to walk down Drew's block on my way. The bus shelter is empty and calling my name, but I don't have my goggles. They were a bad idea from the beginning. I never should've gone in search of binoculars in the first place. But I did learn how to use another technology and see things I never would've seen without them. They were worth it just for finding Frank. I stand at the end of his calm and quiet street. The block has mostly original houses and no apartment buildings, with the brewery at one end. Mature landscaping covering the fences providing natural privacy. Single car driveways that go through to the backyard and detached garages sitting in the corner on the back of each property. Some still have the old school light posts marking their front gate. I stop in the bus shelter and stand facing his house. The first floor lights switch off and a second later the upstairs illuminates. I wonder if he's getting ready for his shower. Will he open his window? Does it matter if someone's watching him or not? Does it matter who's watching him? Does he know it's me?

His window opens and he leans out, gazing toward the bus shelter, "Are you there?" He steps back from his window and pulls his shirt off, then leans out the window grasping the windowsill. I get my phone out and zoom as much as I can. "I see some light, but... Hoodie girl?"

I fumble my phone, dropping it at the sheer surprise of his words. I squeal unintentionally at my clumsiness and duck out of his sight searching for my phone in the dark.

"Everything okay down there?"

I find my phone and stay low, scurrying out of the bus shelter and off to the Creamery.

I RETURN HOME with a scoop of Bourbon Butter Pecan for Caroline, and a pint of half strawberry and half mango sorbet for me later. I can't remember the walk to the Creamery. After the bus shelter incident, I'd lost my appetite. I walk in and hand Caroline her ice cream and stash mine in the freezer, "I need to try that flavor next time. It smells sweet and smoky."

She wrinkles her nose, "I thought you wanted ice cream."

"I wasn't hungry anymore when I got there," I stop fully aware that she's going to ask me more questions. Fuck it, "I stopped at the bus shelter on my way by. He leaned out the window and asked if hoodie girl was there. I freaked out and ducked out of sight."

"Why would you do that? Seriously!" She stops and her expression changes, "He called you hoodie girl?"

"I'm assuming he was referring to me. There could be another girl watching him from the bus shelter or some better hiding place wearing a hoodie," I say wide-eyed.

Caroline glares at me with a smirk.

"Yea, I'm not one to typically assume but I'm pretty confident about this one," I nod my head.

"You think?" She shakes her head. "Hoodie girl is better than stalker, it's almost endearing." She cocks her head to the side and stares at me, "Do you think he likes being watched?"

I wish she asked the question *Do you think he likes it when you watch him?* instead of generically being watched. I shrug in response, "He was looking for me."

"What would he have done if you responded?"

"No."

"No what?"

"I may be crazy for buying NVGs and watching the professional baseball playing love of my life, but that would be like turning myself in and orange isn't my color," I shake my head emphatically.

"And he did kind of ask you to come over that last night before the road trip. I think he likes you," she nods.

"Who's crazy now? He's never met me. Well, he hasn't said a word to me since our senior year of high school and before that it was always questions about the game. How could he possibly like me?"

"You're cute. Or as he said, adorable."

"What do you want me to do?" I shift my feet and place my hand on my hip.

"Your choices. Your life," she says and walks away.

Not helpful at all. First I'm taking too much risk and now I'm not taking enough? That neon pink eighties workout headband has gotten to her brain. I go to my room and crawl into my bed to read and snuggle with Frank. At least he's sane.

CHAPTER TWENTY-SEVEN

Drew

Finally home and in my own bed, I'm relaxed and content. I turn the TV on to music videos and check in.

Me: I'm home from the road trip.
Mom: Happy you're back home safe.
Me: I'm off tomorrow, may I take you out for dinner?
Mom: You don't have to do that honey.
Mom: I'll make a lasagna and you come over.
Me: Whatever you say. I'll never argue with your lasagna.
Mom: Dinner at 5pm, you know what to do?
Me: Yes, I'll bring the wine.
Mom: Such a good son.

Next point of business, I don't own a tuxedo. I could rent one, but I'd rather have my own. I find a local tux shop and save their contact info to reach out to them during business hours.

Mostly, I'm happy because the girl in the oversized hoodie is back. I still have a stalker. Some would say it's bad, but I like it. I only wish I could take her on a date. How do I get her to run to me instead of running away?

I WAKE up refreshed and appreciative that I have the day off. I hop out of bed and put on a T-shirt and a pair of joggers. I slip into my running shoes and go downstairs to make coffee. If I go to the coffee stand I could run into the hoodie girl or talk to her roommate. What would I say? I walk out the door for the coffee stand considering my question. "So, I don't think I've seen another pair of NVGs around the village." "When did you start doing surveillance?" Then it hit me, what if someone is paying her to watch me? I've assumed she likes me, but she might be doing a job. Who would want me watched?

I walk up to the coffee stand, and there's a young guy behind the counter. He stares at me and his eyes get big. I've seen this reaction before—"Drew Brandt! Wow!"

I ignore his enthusiasm, "Hi, can I get a coffee?"

"Of course! What size? House blend?" He asks like I have an answer.

"Whatever the woman with the neon pink headband would make."

He covers his ears. "I forgot my workout gear this morning. I never remember when I'm covering her day off."

He appears genuinely distressed, "I'm sure the customers don't mind."

"Caroline would make you a house blend, and I'm sorry

mine never comes out as good as hers. I don't have a clue what kind of magic she uses." He leans toward me and whispers, "She's a coffee whisperer." He gazes around to make sure nobody heard him.

"I'm sure your coffee will be fine," I nod, trying to get him to move on with it.

"Sure. Sure. Go ahead and pay on the notepad," he says and turns to make my coffee.

I wonder if the hoodie girl gets her coffee here on days that her roommate is off? She might get coffee made for her at home. I pay for my coffee and stand aside waiting while on the look-out. Would I recognize her without her hoodie? She could walk right by me.

"Mr. Brandt? Your coffee is ready." The young man calls out from behind the counter.

"Thank you," I take a sip and leave a buck in his tip jar. I question if it's the same coffee or something else he brewed, but I don't want to engage him again.

I walk home without any sightings of my girl and immediately move on to my errands for the day—wine and tuxedo. Sounds like I've got a fancy night out planned, when in reality it's my favorite lasagna and an evening with my mom.

CHAPTER TWENTY-EIGHT

Maggie

I t's not often that Caroline and I have the same day off, but today is one of those days. We walked over to the other side of the village for breakfast and ordered a Dutch baby. We sit sipping coffee while we wait for our order.

"I've been thinking everything through and all of the signs point to he likes you. So, we need to make a plan for you to meet."

"I've been thinking too and if I screw this up I will lose my job, which provides data for my thesis, most likely have to move due to the distance on the restraining order, probably never be able to attend another baseball game, and I may get arrested and have to serve time in jail."

"Well, if you get arrested you can forget about your thesis so losing the job that provides the data won't mean anything at that point." Caroline stares into my eyes, "The part I'm worried about—"

"Is having to move. I know," I sigh.

"No, I was thinking about you. I'm worried that you will miss out on your opportunity for true love. It's possible he's your one and loves you back. What if that's all true and you never get to find out? Huge risk."

"How do we find that out without me getting arrested?"

"Technicality."

"For you maybe. All you have to do is find a new roommate."

"Are you listening to me? I believe he's interested in you."

"I totally screwed up and will always be the hoodie girl stalker. I should never have done surveillance."

"Who are you kidding? You were out there cock watching."

"Not at the beginning. He did that all on his own."

"Did you zoom in or turn away?"

"I don't see how that is pertinent information."

"Of course you don't."

"You know if you want me to move out you just have to ask, you don't have to get me arrested."

"I'm just trying to be supportive. I've given up judgmental. Though I don't want to be an accessory to your crime, so don't implicate me."

"How about his crime? He did whack it in his window."

"You can use that in your defense statement."

"I'm sorry, your honor, I didn't want to be rude and leave the show he was putting on before he was finished?"

"He won't want anyone to know about that. That's your safety net! If he wants to get you arrested, threaten to report his show to the press."

"And after I've blackmailed him, run off happily into the sunset with him? I don't think so."

"It's true, everyone doesn't take kindly to blackmail. Hmmm."

"I need to leave it alone. I need to give it some time and maybe next season start sitting up front for batting practice every day and go from there. No more bus shelter time for me. No more goggles."

"It's possible."

FOR THE NEXT few days I immerse myself in my thesis. Sleep, thesis, game, repeat. No unnecessary shenanigans. Well, all shenanigans are unnecessary. No shenanigans. No goggles. No night time strolls.

I set my alarm for Saturday morning and do my hair for the banquet before the game starts. It's an early game day with an odd Saturday start time of 1pm. It happens some-times—usually because they want to televise the game as one of the games of the week. It works for me because my banquet is tonight at 7pm. I should be home by 5pm to touch up my hair and change into my dress and heels.

CHAPTER TWENTY-NINE

Drew

"What's got you all pouty?" Martin asks as we do an early morning run along the San Diego Bay.

"Pouty?"

"Yeah, like a little girl who lost her kitten. It's got to be the chick. How's the stalker?"

"She was watching me the night we got back from the road trip, but it didn't look like she had her NVGs with her. That's it, haven't seen her since."

"Maybe she's on vacation."

"Maybe she was doing surveillance for somebody else and the job is over."

"She doesn't seem like someone that would take jobs watching people."

"Point is that neither of us know her. She could be a federal agent."

"What did you do?"

"What are you talking about?"

"Why would a federal agent be watching you unless you did something? I've never heard of them providing security for professional athletes. Maybe their capture rate is low this year and they figure athletes do some stupid shit, so as long as they watch long enough they'll get something so they can swoop in and arrest you."

"They're watching the wrong player."

"I'd have said the same thing until your naked-in-the-window stunt. They didn't arrest you, so I don't think she's a federal agent. I suppose there's a slight chance she's waiting for you to do something worse."

"No, I think you're right. She wouldn't get caught off guard if she was a federal agent."

"You really want to date the stalker chick?" Martin asks as we walk into the locker room.

"Yes."

He shakes his head at me in disbelief as we change for batting practice. I check my locker and I'm happy to see my tuxedo has been delivered. I'll have limited time after the game to get ready for the banquet and not enough time to go home.

CHAPTER THIRTY

Maggie

Present Day...

I've arrived at the banquet and I'm attempting to make my rounds, talking to all of the department heads and especially my advisor. I have all evening to get it done, and it gives me a goal to focus on rather than standing around bored. Standing? These sparkly peekaboos are elegant and second nature to me after Caroline kept reminding me to wear them all week. I'm actually enjoying being dressed up like an adult with my hair done and makeup on. It's nice to get together with all of my colleagues from across the science departments and enjoy an evening of intelligent conversation, food, and music.

I take a glass of champagne from a waiter circulating with a tray full. I sip it slowly to make it last and not be the only one without a drink. I'm not against a drink. It's not the time or place for it. Basically, I'm at a work party and need to maintain the respect of my supervisors. I'm not one to cut loose, but either way I need to maintain a level head.

My advisor walks up to me and extends her hand, "Hi, I'm Professor Joan Wilhelm from the Department of Math and Statistics. Thank you for joining us this evening. This is how we keep our departments going and support our students in their progressing research."

I smile and try to hold back my giggle, "Hi Professor Wilhelm." I wink, "Is the fundraiser portion of the evening going well?" Has it been that long since I visited my advisor?

She takes a step back, staring at me, "Ms. Hamilton?"

I nod and raise my eyebrows.

"You look very nice this evening. I was so proud to see you on the honoree list. I can't believe I didn't recognize you, though I don't think I've ever seen you with your hair down, or in a skirt and heels. It suits you, you're a gorgeous young woman."

My cheeks warm, "I don't know about that. I just wanted to be dressed appropriately for the event to show my respect and appreciation for being honored."

Professor Wilhelm leans in, "We're honoring you because you're exemplary, don't underestimate yourself in any way."

"Thank you, Professor Wilhelm," my confidence level rises.

"Now, go shock some of the male professors. See how many recognize you or ask you on a date!" She chuckles as she walks away.

I'm not tempting fate with her challenge.

The head of the College of Science steps up to the podium, "Welcome all to our annual Researching the Sciences banquet. There are many pieces to this evening, but most importantly we're here to support our students in progressing their education and their research. Many of our honorees tonight are post-graduate students who I will be introducing to you individually throughout the evening. I'd like to thank you all for being here and for your support, and please welcome our distinguished guests from the community: The County of San Diego's Educational Liaison, our own university president, San Diego's Chief of Police, Commander of Fire Battalion 4, Balboa Park Board President, and I believe I just saw him walk in, Drew Brandt from the San Diego Seals, who was a student here not too many years ago and graduated with a minor in Physics. Enjoy your evening everyone and may you be loose with your pocketbooks!"

Drew Brandt? Drew's here? Here? I calmly turn, wanting to find him, but not wanting to be obvious about it. Oh my god, he's wearing a tux! He's so fucking hot! My vision of him gives him his own backlit glow. I keep turning not wanting to give away my dumbfounded expression or have him catch me staring at him—which I absolutely would do. He's smiling and waving at people who are trying to get his attention from around the room. The band starts to play and I focus on them, trying not to spend the evening wondering if the police will be barging through the door to arrest me. A hand pats my shoulder.

"Dance with me?" He asks turning me toward him, smiling from ear to ear. His warm deep voice causes echoes through my body.

No is on the tip of my tongue, I don't dance unless I'm in my own bedroom alone and nobody can see me. Then I remember what my advisor said, "I'd love to." I say it and gaze up at the man I'm dancing with to find Drew Brandt. I don't remember him being this much taller than me. He's so much taller than me, even in my high-heels. Standing this close to him my brain is running in every direction. I've never been so aware of how naked I am in this dress. His hand is respectfully on my side with fingers extended across my bare back. His warm fingers graze against my skin like a match against a striker.

"You look beautiful this evening," he says with a friendly smile. "I'm sure you're beautiful every day."

Is he hitting on me? Does he recognize me?

"I'm sorry, I didn't introduce myself. My name is Drew."

"I know who you are. Everyone knows who you are."

"Oh, are you a baseball fan?"

Does he really not know who I am? "My whole life, I grew up watching games with my dad."

"A Seals fan?" He smiles.

"Since birth." I confirm and nod.

"Me, too," he replies. "It's like playing for my dream team. I couldn't be prouder than when I put my Seals uniform on each day. You ever have that dream that comes true?"

You're in it right now. "It's surreal and all you can do is hope it's as good as the dream." Please let him be as good as my dream. Good god don't let him be the letdown of my life.

"We tend to build things up in our heads and that makes it hard to live up to, but being the second baseman for the Seals has been more than I ever imagined."

He's articulate and well-spoken on the fly, not just for interviews. He can even talk while he dances and he's leading. I don't have to be a dancer, I can simply follow him. I remember my prom and that guy couldn't dance, didn't lead, kind of stood there holding my hand while I attempted to do something like dance. Drew is light on his feet, coordinated, and moves without any effort. Of course he does. He's an athlete.

"Are you a professor?" He asks.

"Oh no, I'm a post-grad student."

"Which science department are you in."

"Math and Statistics."

"Interesting field."

"I enjoy working with numbers."

"You better in that department," he chuckles and spins me around.

Careful with my words, I'm waiting to find out if he recognizes me before I give anything away. Quietly absorbing his closeness and committing it to memory. His masculine yet tender hands. His clean man scent. His confidence enveloping me. He's not going to recognize me, but if he does at least I'll have the memory to replay in my head.

CHAPTER THIRTY-ONE

Drew

Walking into the Researching the Sciences banquet to find this gorgeous, familiar creature is unexpected. She's not the counterpart to the old guys in sport coats and corduroy I'd conjured in my head. She's the shining light of elegance, beauty, and confidence—everyone else in the room is in the shadow of her vibrance.

She's so familiar, yet I can't place who she is. I'm here to represent the Seals, and I can't take my eyes off of her. I should be mingling and chatting up everyone in attendance, but I walk directly to her and without a thought I ask her to dance. She had hesitance in her eyes that cleared quickly like a storm just passing through. With her hand in mine I immediately felt at peace, as if my missing piece had been found and the puzzle was now complete. Except I'm missing some facts, I can't remember who she is. I tried introducing myself, hoping she'd reciprocate—she didn't. Standing closer to her, I'm taken by her. Such poise in a respectable yet sexy dress and heels that bring her up to my chin. My fingers find her skin, her dress is backless and I want to hold onto her tightly and pull her into me, but it's not the place. I gaze down into her warm green eyes and read my future. This is crazy. Something needs to give me more, tell me who she is! I hold onto her and keep dancing as the band continues to play. She allows it without complaint. Could she be getting the same connection?

The head of the College of Sciences goes to the podium and when the song is over he speaks, "I'm glad everyone is enjoying the band and cocktails. I'd like to take a moment to introduce you to one of our honorees. Maya Plottz is a postgraduate in our chemistry program with research comparing the chemical compounds of sugar to other natural and man-made sweeteners. She hopes to find another natural sweetener that is a healthier option for people overall and especially those who are diabetic. She plans to continue research surrounding diabetic needs and lifestyle when she completes her education." A young woman joins him at the podium and shakes his hand. "I'll announce more honorees throughout the evening. Thank you." The crowd politely applauds.

The music starts again and I refuse to let her go, gazing into her eyes for acceptance. She smiles in return, and my heart skips a beat. We dance with her hand in mind silently until the next honoree announcement. As the Head of the College of Sciences speaks I lean into her ear, "I'm going to get a drink. What would you like?"

"I have a glass of champagne already," she replies and points to where she left it to find an empty table.

I nod, "I'll fix that." I stare at her for a moment, trying to figure out who she is and smooth my thumb over her soft hand. Reluctantly I release her hand to retrieve drinks and antipasto. I'd love to drag her off into a corner somewhere to sit and talk, but that's not the mission tonight. I need to remember I'm here to represent the Seals.

I put on my game face and shake hands with everyone as I walk across the room, stopping to sign a few baseballs along the way. I always find it interesting how people have base-balls with them in the most unexpected places—like the Researching the Sciences banquet. Then again, the Seals have probably sent players before, so maybe they anticipated the opportunity. I'm happy to do it, nothing makes me prouder than being a Seal and helping my community. I find the antipasto and wonder what she likes. I commandeer a tray I find sitting with only a couple glasses of champagne left on it, and add a selection of the antipastos. I turn to find her and she's worked her way to the far other side of the room.

CHAPTER THIRTY-TWO

Maggie

I was dancing with Drew. Of all the things I've never imagined doing. Dancing with my hand in his. His strong lead giving me confidence on the dance floor. He hasn't asked my name or questioned me on surveillance tactics. He also hasn't returned when he said he was going to get a drink. I've used that excuse to get out of a conversation before. It's fine. Back to my original plan, I need to make my rounds and be seen by the department heads.

As I start my way through the crowd Professor Wilhelm approaches, "Weren't you dancing with the baseball player?"

"Yes, I was."

"Why did you let him go?"

"I'm here for the event, not for a man."

She quirks her eyes sideways, "You're here, that's enough for the event. Don't waste opportunities."

"This is an opportunity for me to reinforce my relationships with the department heads and make sure they know this is important to me. I'll be presenting my thesis soon and I want them to remember me."

"That's an admirable plan. You've always been studious. It's important to have balance in your life. I have every confidence that your thesis will be unique, factually supported, and thought provoking. Considering your topic, you'll probably get offers to work for multiple sports franchises. When you make your choices, choose what makes you happy." She searches across the room to find Drew, "I wouldn't let go of that tall drink of water." She winks and walks away.

Regardless, he's busy on the other side of the room or has chosen to ditch me. I move forward, talking to those that mean the most to my future first. Shaking hands and discussing my progress. It's refreshing to discuss my thesis from a scientific point of view with people who understand it, though they don't understand what Moneyball is nor some of the baseball statistics. I suppose I'm unique like Professor Wilhelm said.

The head of the College of Sciences announces the next honoree and I'm starting to believe my flippant thoughts. Did he ditch me? He's here as a public figure. I'm here as a postgrad student. We both have jobs to do. That's all that's going on here. I've already gotten more than I ever expected from him and the night overall. I need to keep it what it is and stay out of my head. A man asked me to dance and I danced with him. That's it. Nothing more. Nothing less. I'm sure it happens to women all the time and it doesn't come with other attachments. Simply a dance partner. The problem is that I want to dance with him and only him and naked would be even better. I can't be thinking like that. I can't consider going home with him, it's not even a date. It's probably what he's used to or even expects being a baseball player. No, don't put traditional athlete stigmas on Drew. He's not that guy. I believe it in my heart and soul that he's different, a family man maybe. Woah. Do I want a family? I shake my head to clear the thought.

I turn to observe as the band starts to play again and find Drew standing near the dance floor with his hands full, scanning the room. I should go back to him, but what if he's not searching for me? *Never waste an opportunity...* I guess there's only one way to find out. I walk up to him and place my hand on his upper arm. I've always wanted to do that, and discover the tension in his muscles.

He turns to me immediately, "I lost you."

"I found you," I say simply.

He hands me a flute of champagne, "I brought you a bite to eat, well one of each of them so you could choose."

"Thank you," I say and choose the mini flatbread with a sun-dried tomato on it.

He points to another with raw veggies sticking out of it, "This one's good if you like hummus."

I dip a carrot in and give it a taste, "That's tasty."

He takes a drink of his champagne and stares at me, "Shall we dance some more?"

I nod anxious to get his hands back on me. The music stops again before we can get started and the head of the College of Sciences speaks, "Our next honoree is Margaret Hamilton. She's a post-grad student working in our Math and Statistics Department with an incomparable knack for numbers. She's currently working on research that combines two of her favorite things, statistics and baseball. I was just talking to her advisor and I'm told her thesis is titled, "Skill, Chemistry, or Moneyball," and I can't wait to read it. Her extensive knowledge in the two unique areas make her invaluable to the sports world. This woman is going to make lots of money helping a team win championships, and hopefully she comes back to share with her peers." He gestures to me and I walk to the podium beaming at his words. I never thought of it that way. Sports money has never been my goal. That my advisor and her peers foresee what's to come excites me. And people say they don't know what learning math will do to help them in the real world. I shake his hand and pose for photos as I thank him for his kind words.

CHAPTER THIRTY-THREE

Drew

Margaret Hamilton? Hold on. That name... she's the girl from my yearbook! She was our score-keeper in high school and college. My mom left a sticky note saying I should date her. She wanted to hang out and I didn't pay attention. She's a friend from my past. I'm going out on a limb here and saying she fits the requirements Martin set for me. She's in the yearbooks like Carter suggested, and then she's magically here. I hate to come off as a hopeless romantic, but it's as if it's meant to be. Plus, she's beautiful, smart, and has goals. Yea, she ticks all the boxes.

I stare at her full of pride for her accomplishments. To be chosen from hundreds of potential honorees is something to be proud of. The best of the best in her department, and she definitely stands out in the crowd. I make eye contact with her and clap along with the rest of the room. Her smile brightens as she gazes at me.

The music starts playing again as she walks away from

the podium. I reach my hand out toward her and she gives me a slight nod, but she's stopped by people congratulating her. I watch as she shakes hands and accepts hugs with a glow about her.

She approaches and I grab her, pulling her in tight for a hug, "I'm so proud of you. I didn't know you were being honored tonight." The fit of her body against mine surprises and arouses me. My nostrils fill with her intoxicating feminine scent, a light musky mix of fresh citrus and coconut with some floral notes. Her body tenses and I wonder if I've gone too far. She's perfect in my arms. I discover I'm still squeezing her and release my hold. "I don't think I've seen you since my last college baseball game."

"I see you all the time, I watch all of the Seals games."

"I've been living for the game and concentrating on making myself a better player in any way that I can. Not taking any time for me," I smooth my thumb over her hand. "I'm trying to do something for me and find time for a life outside of the Seals."

"It's important to have balance," she says.

"Is that so?"

"Yes," she nods. "I allow myself quiet time for reading almost every day. It's time for me to do something I enjoy."

What do I do for me? I enjoy my projects, like getting the property updated. I want to learn more about her. "I'd love to hear more about your thesis. Skill, Chemistry, or Moneyball sounds like a comparison or maybe a balancing game."

Her eyes brighten with clarity, "In a way." She stops and waits for me to signal her before she continues. "I believe the optimized team has a necessary combination of all three. Most teams don't see the value of personal connections on the team, and though I'm all about the statistics I believe that what happens on the field is not all reflected in the standard game averages." Her tone and body language change becoming more technical and professional.

"It sounds interesting. I'm sure I have my own point of view being on the field and in the club house, but there's not many of us in that position. I'd love to hear more. Maybe over breakfast or coffee?" I chuckle and clarify, "My baseball schedule doesn't allow me time to take you out to dinner until November." I grin hoping she understands since she's a baseball fan.

"I love coffee," she replies and I have the sense that she was going to say more, but doesn't.

"Perfect," I find myself wondering if she's taken and I just overstepped my boundaries more than once.

CHAPTER THIRTY-FOUR

Maggie

I need Caroline. The champagne is going straight through me, but also straight to my head. Less words are better. He remembers me, which I can't imagine why or how he could possibly remember me. It doesn't seem like he's connected me to the adorable hoodie girl or the stalker, but he could be keeping that to himself. I don't want to lie to him, but I also don't want to give too much away. I stop mid-thought realizing that... yes... I think he just asked me out and I haven't responded other than confirming that I like coffee. What if he wants to take me to Caroline's coffee stand? Oh my gosh, I could offer to get a drink with him after the game. The stand is closed then. That could go haywire. He could interpret that in any number of ways including that I'm offering to go to his place and, well, I've already seen what he does when he gets home for the night, not to mention that he's invited me in. Though, again, we can't be sure he was inviting me and not somebody else wearing an oversized hoodie. Shit! I still haven't answered him and now his eyes are a bit squinchy, "Coffee would be splendid." Coffee would be splendid? Splendid? Now I'm channeling a character from one of my historical romance books. Before he can say anything else, "Please excuse me." I gesture toward the ladies' room and walk right past it to get outside for a breath of fresh air.

I walk around the corner of the building and lean against the brick wall. Suddenly realizing I'm dressed for the event and not in my jeans, I stand up straight and pull myself away from the building to find myself—stuck. Mother fucker! I dial Caroline and pull harder.

"Hello. Is this the amazing Margaret Hamilton, sought after statistician and future infamous baseball prognosticator?" Caroline answers with fervor.

I admit it makes me smile, but it doesn't resolve my situation, "Help. Please. I'm out of my range here with him and I'm stuck and I'm not knowledgeable in men or clothes," I pull harder extracting myself from the building as something attached to me rips. "Damn it!"

"Okay. Okay. Deep breath, Mags," Caroline simulates the breath I should be taking audibly from the other end of the phone line.

"I was doing so well. I'd stretched the glass of champagne. I was making rounds to talk to all of the department heads and my advisor, exactly like I'd planned and then *he* showed up."

"How's your outfit going over?"

"Oh, totally amazing. My advisor didn't even recognize me."

"Perfect! You're a rock star."

"Except I'm not a rock star because I'm outside and I have no idea what part of anything I ripped but I'm getting a draft in a personal place that I wasn't getting before. AAhhh-hhh! And I left him standing there pretending to go to the bathroom. What am I, 12?" I screech.

"First, quiet down so nobody can hear you. What he are you talking about?"

"Who do you think?"

"That professor with the bad toupee that you absolutely hate? The campus police officer that chats you up all the time? Throw me a bone here."

"Drew."

"Drew Brandt is there?"

"Yup."

"Any signs at all of someone preparing to arrest you?"

"Nope. But he walked up to me and took my hand and we danced and it was the most amazing thing in the world to have his hands on me. I'll never dance with anyone else ever again. He made me confident on the dance floor."

"I'm sorry, did you just refer to yourself as confident in a sentence with the words dance floor in it?"

"Shut up. Yes. Will you please focus here? This is serious."

"Okay. One thing at a time. Is your dress hiked up letting the breeze in?"

"No."

"Pantyhose. My bet is you snagged your pantyhose. The fluffy outer layer of your dress getting ripped wouldn't cause a draft for your promised land and the inner layer of the dress was protected by the outer layer."

"That's fine and dandy—how do I fix it?"

"Reach down between your legs and find the hole."

"Caroline, this isn't the time nor place for kinky shenanigans!"

"Get your head in the game! The hole in your pantyhose. Stop daydreaming about Drew's cock."

"I was not...," I stop because I was. "It's going to look suspicious me standing outside with my hands between my legs."

"Do I have to give you step by step instructions? Go to the bathroom and lock yourself in one of the stalls. Just take me with you and let me know when we're locked into a bathroom stall."

"You don't have to be mean."

"I'm not being mean."

"Wait. What if Drew sees me going into the bathroom?"

"Which do you prefer Drew seeing you walk into the bathroom or Drew seeing your hoohaw?"

I hesitate considering my options, then answer, "I'm interested in Drew seeing my hoohaw but not until after a reasonable amount of time has passed. What's the standard, 3 dates? 6 dates?"

"Okay, so we've determined that Drew isn't allowed to see your hoohaw tonight. Will you please just get your ass into the bathroom? And remember, most likely nobody can see the rip and if they can they aren't looking for it so they won't notice when you walk through the room filled with people."

"Thanks for that."

"Anytime."

I search the room for Drew as I approach the bathroom door. He's facing the other direction in a conversation with the head of the College of Science. I slide into the bathroom and into the first stall, locking it behind me, "Okay, in the stall and door is locked."

"Pee."

"I'm sorry?"

"That's what you do when you're in a bathroom stall. Pee."

"Yes, but..."

"Pull your pantyhose down and find the snag."

"This would be a lot easier if I was sitting down."

"What did I just tell you to do?"

"Shut up. I can't help it. You don't understand. The man of my dreams approached me, told me I'm beautiful, and twirled me around the dance floor with his big warm baseball playing man hands on me."

"Do you think he knows who you are?"

"He knows my name and that I was his scorekeeper when he was younger. That's all I know for sure. He's acting like he remembers me from my college scorekeeping days."

"So, we need to burn all of your oversized hoodies and you can never wear one again, he'll never know."

"Did I mention he asked me out?"

"That's a kind of important piece you left out. You said yes, right?"

"I said I love coffee and I said coffee would be splendid. Then I needed you and here we are."

"Are you sure you're not missing any other important details?"

"No. Help me."

"Did you find the snag?"

"No, I'm wrestling with the pantyhose to get them off. Who wears these things? Why did I need the control tops?"

"It's your foundation and doesn't matter if you're already slender, it smooths out your silhouette. Slow down, it will make it easier. Take a deep breath."

"I'm lucky I'm breathing at all," I say as I roll my pantyhose down and pee. "Shit."

"What?"

"They're snagged from my knee to my crotch, all the way up my inner thigh."

"Okay, do you have any hair spray or nail polish?"

"No, I'm not here to do salon work!"

"Okay, then take them off. Ditch them completely. Don't flush them, they clog toilets."

"They don't seem like they'd clog a toilet."

"I thought the same, and I can tell you they do."

"How do I not know about this?"

"Don't ask questions. We need to get you through tonight and back into that hot baseball player's arms."

"Yes, ma'am!"

"Slide the pantyhose off while you sit on the toilet. Take one shoe off at a time, then take them off your foot, sliding your foot back into your shoe without touching the nasty bathroom floor. Then repeat."

"Okay."

"Wipe and get off the toilet. Make sure your dress is pulled down and the outer layer isn't sticking out crazy. That's what the bathroom mirror is for. Double check to make sure you don't have toilet paper stuck to you anywhere."

"I know how to use the bathroom."

"One can never be too sure in the middle of a crisis. Wash your hands. Make sure that you still look good overall and strut back out there to claim your prey."

"Okay. Thank you," I hang up on Caroline and walk out of the bathroom with confidence.

I survey the room to find everyone is leaving and the room is half empty. No sign of Drew. I open my phone to call Caroline and realize I was on the phone with her for half an hour. He left.

CHAPTER THIRTY-FIVE

Drew

The music stops and everyone is leaving, but there's no Margaret. I hang out as long as I can without being one of the last people in the building, and thank the head of the College of Sciences for having me, handing him a generous personal donation to the Math and Statistics Department.

I may have overstepped my boundaries. I didn't ask if she's available and it would make sense that she's not. A beautiful and intelligent woman like her should be spoken for and have a line of men hoping the current man in her life fucks up so they can get their chance. It's times like this when I realize how much being a professional baseball player has affected me. From the moment I saw her, I never once considered that I couldn't have her. She's already mine. Except, she's not. If she was mine, I'd never let her go and I'd make sure she never had a reason to want to.

Walking to my car I wonder why she didn't say goodbye. Fuck, I didn't get her number. I hope she's okay.

CHAPTER THIRTY-SIX

Maggie

I walk in the door at home, slamming it behind me.

"I didn't expect you to be home that quick," Caroline calls out from the kitchen.

I stand in the kitchen doorway with my high heels dangling off my fingertips, "Drew left. No sign of him anywhere when I came out of the bathroom."

"Can I just say that I love that dress on you and you really need to wear your hair down like that more often?"

"You just did. It doesn't solve my missing baseball player problem."

"He's not missing. You know exactly where he is and where to find him every day."

"He was supposed to be there when I came out of the bathroom waiting to sweep me off my feet and lead me back out onto the dance floor. He was supposed to hold me tight against him and gaze at me like I'm the only woman in the world. He was supposed to spread his hands across my bare back and send shocks through my body with a graze of his fingertips."

"Anything else? Was he supposed to have a magical carriage to take you away to a fantasy land where little white mice do all of your chores?"

"No!"

"Okay, sorry. What am I missing here?" She asks in a calm tone and places her hand on my shoulder.

"He did all of those things and he was going to do them again, yet the universe made it stop."

"Maybe the universe didn't make it stop, maybe it just hit the brakes a little."

"What do you mean?"

"You aren't sure how to handle the situation anyway. You called me and told me yourself that you're out of your depth. I think you need a plan."

"I still don't know if he knows or what he knows or how he'll respond when he finds out."

"Why does he have to find out?"

"Eventually, he'll find out. I don't want that hanging over me. I don't want to be waiting for the second shoe to finally fall and ruin it all."

"If it's meant to be, nothing can ruin it."

"Then what's the plan? I don't have his number. He doesn't know that I have his address and work at the stadium. I can find him. Waiting for him to find me? That might never happen."

"First, where do we stand on burning the hoodies?"

"I'm not burning my hoodies."

"Would you consider boxing them up and hiding them in a closet for the foreseeable future?"

"How will I stay warm and comfortable without my hoodies?"

"Layers and a jacket. Maybe some more feminine options?"

I see the glint in her eyes, "I don't have the money for a new wardrobe and I like my hoodies. Like I said, he's going to figure it out eventually."

"Can we get you nestled permanently into his heart before that happens?"

"This sounds like a bad idea. Secrets in a relationship are bad juju."

"So, if it comes up tell him and don't hide it, but don't offer it up on a silver platter either."

"I don't know."

"Do you want back in his arms or not?"

"Can I keep my hoodie?"

"How about a compromise? Box up the oversized hoodies and wear the ones that actually fit?"

I reach out my hand and we shake on it.

"Good. I'd like you to consider wearing your hair down and sitting field level for batting practice. Maybe not tomorrow, but soon."

"I can do that."

"No baggy jeans either."

"Fine. Am I trying to be seen?"

"Yes."

It's my dream all over again. Tomorrow is a day game. No batting practice. Maybe Monday.

CHAPTER THIRTY-SEVEN

Drew

Walking into the stadium early on Sunday morning I stop at Carter's office and knock on the open door.

"Good morning," he says without a glance in my direction.

"Good morning. I'm wondering if you can help me find somebody."

He stops and turns to me, "What's going on? I'm not a private investigator. That's way above my pay grade."

"No, she's a Seals fan. Maybe a ticket holder or some connection that would allow us her contact information?"

"Tell me more."

"I ran into a woman at the banquet last night and I lost her before I could get her number. I went to school with her. I found her in my yearbooks."

"I told you yearbooks would be helpful."

"Yes, and you were right. Also, my mom loved going

through my yearbooks before she dropped them off for me. She even left me sticky notes with commentary."

"Why haven't we seen your mom at a game?"

"She thinks it's my work and not a place for moms."

"I'll work on that."

"Anyway, the woman's name is Margaret Hamilton."

"That sounds awfully familiar. Let me see what I can do," he nods.

"Thank you," I say and continue into the locker room. I shouldn't be so interested. It's possible she ditched me on purpose last night, but I don't believe that.

Martin high fives me as I walk into the locker room, "Quick stadium run before the gates open?"

"Let's do it," I change into my cutoff shorts and the new workout T-shirt that was left in my locker for me that says, "Seals slide in for the steal," with our cartoon mascot on it keeping his tail fin on the base, and put on my running shoes. "We have time for up and back," I nod at Martin and we walk to the tunnel door, taking time to stretch against the wall. At the end of the tunnel we open the door to daylight and run up the six-level switchback ramp to the upper deck. Following our typical path, we run to the far end then up and down the steps between every section of seats. The upper section has steeper steps, so we get a better workout. We stop and stand along the outer railing enjoying the cool breeze off the bay.

"I like your focus today, another level of drive. What's going on?" Martin questions.

"I met a woman at the banquet last night who's everything I told you I want," I stop a moment.

Martin nods.

"Let me rephrase that, I reconnected with a woman who

I went to school with," I grin uncontrollably remembering her beautiful smile and the softness of her skin.

"Reconnected, like hooked up?"

"No. We never dated or anything. She was our team scorekeeper. But she knew me before professional baseball, she's gorgeous, and she's a post-grad working on her thesis."

"Interesting. She knows our sport, she's actively working on achieving her educational goals, and she's as nerdy as you," he pokes at me.

"She could be perfect," I nod.

"What's wrong with her?"

"I asked her to coffee and I didn't get her number."

"Man, you always get the digits."

"She kind of disappeared on me. She went to the ladies' room and I never saw her again."

"Don't take it personal. Shit happens. She might be in a relationship and need to break it off before she can date you."

"Or she might be happily taken and not interested."

"Naw, they all want a baseball player, even the ones who say they don't," he replies in his cocky way.

"Don't you think that's assuming a lot? Just because we're baseball players doesn't mean we can have whoever we want."

"We can have almost whoever we want. Look, give her some time and if she's interested she knows where to find you."

"She does know where to find me. She's a Seals fan."

"There you go. What happened with the stalker chick?"

"No signs of her."

"Dodged a bullet with that one. The woman from last night sounds like a better option anyway. More stable, less likely to pound on your door screaming at midnight."

"Absolutely a more logical choice," I say wondering about the adorable hoodie girl.

We jog down the ramp for our cool down and walk the main concourse before going back down to the tunnel. The tunnel runs most of the way around the stadium and is only accessible for employees, barring the occasional guided tour of the stadium. It's concrete with paint on the walls, and not brightly lit. There are golf cart type maintenance vehicles driving through it frequently transporting people and things to different areas of the stadium.

There's a spread of fresh fruit, omelets, and English muffins getting delivered to the club house as we walk in. Perfect way to spend the time we have left before the game.

CHAPTER THIRTY-EIGHT

Maggie

I wake up to the amazing smell of pancakes and coffee, and wonder what's going on. It must be Caroline's day off. I pull myself out of the layers of blankets I'm wrapped in and get a squealing protest from Frank. I pick him up and pet his head, setting him down in a good nesting spot on my blanket covered pillow. I pull on my fleece-lined leggings and wander out to the kitchen in a well-worn over-sized Seals shirt.

Caroline smiles at me as I walk into the kitchen and hands me a cup of coffee, "Good morning. I thought you should be fed and caffeinated before you go to the stadium today to help keep you focused and on track without distractions."

I sip and nod as I remember last night, "You really do make the best coffee."

"Thank you," she sets a plate of pancakes on our small

kitchen table with a fork. "Syrup is warmed and waiting in the microwave."

I grab the syrup and some butter, and sit happily inhaling my pancakes.

She joins me a few minutes later with a plate of her own, "We need to go through your clothes and figure out what's acceptable for the plan we agreed on last night."

"I think I can figure that out on my own."

She glares at me and takes a deep breath, "You're an adult who is capable of dressing herself. Are you sure we can't burn your oversized hoodies to make sure you don't wear one of them on accident?"

"We aren't going to burn anything. That's how I stay warm. I'm not changing myself for a man."

"How about to stay out of jail and for a man?" She gazes into the nothingness and holds her hand up likes she's reading a headline in Times Square, "World renowned statistician famous for championship baseball teams across the globe arrested by police on stalking and voyeur charges associated with divorce papers filed by her professional baseball player husband."

"How is pretending not to be me going to help? I'm not a voyeur. I understand how I could be considered a stalker."

"Did you or did you not watch him whack off naked in the shower?"

"You were there. I didn't expect him to, or ask him to do that. That's all on him."

"I don't think the jury will see it that way."

"He hasn't even kissed me yet and you've already got us divorcing?"

"Hear me out. There's no way you forget about him. He's been in your heart for way too long for that to happen, and, after last night, he probably left you wanting more. Though I was happy to hear you don't want him to see your hoohaw yet."

"Thank you. I do have standards."

"You're welcome. However, I still think you need to wear clothes that fit and show your feminine side. This includes no oversized hoodies outside of our apartment."

"Is this a ploy to get me to do laundry?"

"No. You agreed to box up the oversized hoodies. We shook on it."

If Frank finds that box he'll never come out. "Okay, so you want me to start going to batting practice dressed on the feminine side with my hair down?"

"Yes, and sit somewhere in his line of sight."

"What about the 'adorable hoodie girl?'"

"I thought about that. It's risky. The stalker is hoodie girl, too. Plus, he was obviously interested in you last night and you need to run with it."

"I'm not wearing a dress to the game."

"I don't expect you to. Seals gear is fine, but it needs to fit and you need to do something to your hair besides pull it up into a ponytail."

"I can't work with my hair down."

"I'm sure you can."

"I can't. It gets in the way and messes me up when it falls across my scorebooks."

"Then tie it up into a knot or a bun when you get up to your desk, but not when you're in the stands."

"Okay, I can do that. Does that mean no baseball cap?"

"I think the baseball cap will hide you, but if you have to be in the sun wear your cap. What are you wearing today?"

"Day game and the suns out, so I'm wearing shorts and a Seals shirt."

"How about making today a test run? Wear a feminine

cut shirt instead of those boxy unisex shirts you always wear and your hair down with a tie on your wrist for when you need it?"

"Will you make me another coffee and can I have more pancakes?"

"Yes."

"Deal." I'd be 10 pounds lighter if Caroline wasn't my roommate, but it's worth it.

I UNPACK my backpack and go through everything to make sure I have what I need and nothing I can do without. I leave my big hoodie at home and stuff my lightweight girlie one into my backpack along with my brush and extra hair ties. My laptop is in its pocket along with the cord so I can plug it in. NVGs are on the charger in my bedroom and will be staying there. Frank is already nesting in the big hoodie I just tossed onto my bed. My pencil bag is in the front pocket with my wallet, keys, Air Pods, and stadium ID. I find my notebook on my nightstand and put it in my backpack with my scorebooks. It's lighter overall, that's a positive.

I drop my backpack at the door ready to go and walk through the kitchen as if I were on a catwalk for Caroline's approval.

"Very nice. How do you feel?"

"Comfortable. I can do this" I nod.

"Well, you're absolutely fetching and sporty. I made you another coffee to-go," she smiles and hands me a coffee in a large to-go cup from the coffee stand.

"You love me," I grin.

"Yes I do, even if you need serious help. Enjoy your coffee," she shakes her head at me and laughs.

"Thank you!" I call out to her as I put on my backpack and walk out the door.

Walking to the stadium other potential scenarios cross my mind. What if I run into him on my walk to the stadium? What if I run into him at the stadium? What if I run into him on my walk home? What if they put me on the big screen for some reason? What if we run into each other and he doesn't recognize me? I remind myself that it doesn't matter. The plan is not to hide from him and not to keep secrets, but also don't offer up incriminating information. If I can learn surveillance I can handle this.

I walk with confidence through the employee gate and straight to my desk in time to watch the warm-up and be ready for the game. It's a sunny warm day and I'm glad to be watching from my covered and air-conditioned space. I grab a couple bottles of water and get comfortable at my desk.

The scorekeeper walks in and turns to me, "You look nice today."

"Thank you," I smile in return and get my pencils all laid out next to my scorebooks.

I'm accustomed to blocking out the chatter in the press box, but something has the press guys super chatty today. I put my headphones on to listen to the pregame and block them out, while I get the lineup written into my scorebooks. The batting lineup is slightly different today, but coach kept Martin and Brandt together, and moved Cross from lead off to third right before Seno. He's keeping the duos together, I wonder if he read my notes. Though, I do love Cross as lead-off. A folded piece of paper is slid over to my desk and I open it:

New Girl,
Welcome and thank you for joining us in the press
box. You provide a beautiful and refreshing view. Can
I take you out to dinner tonight? Kind of a welcome to
your new job thing.
Jake (Associated Sports Press)

What the fuck? I've been here for over a season already. I fold the note back up and leave it sitting there. The score-keeper turns to me and chuckles, I make a frustrated face at him and shake my head. I turn back to get to business and there are two more notes left on my desk.

Hey beautiful,
Where did you come from to brighten my life? I'd love
to get to know you better. Maybe coffee sometime?
John (San Diego Baseball News)

Welcome,
The press box would like to invite you to happy hour
after the game, as a meet & greet in your honor.
Press Box

I keep up with the score and the game, and there's a challenge under review in the first inning. I text Caroline:

Me: WTF is going on?
Me: The press box reporters all think I'm new here.
Me: I've got an invitation to dinner, an invitation to coffee, and they want to take me to happy hour to welcome me to the press box.
Caroline: LOL
Me: This isn't a laughing matter.

Me: What's wrong with these guys? I've been here over a
year.
Caroline: You were hidden.
Me: I was right here in the same place the whole time.
Caroline: SMH you were hidden in that oversized hoodie!
Caroline: Your hair down. Clothes that fit properly. A
whole new woman.
Me: Seriously?
Caroline: Yep.
Caroline: Did you tie your hair up yet?
Me: No. But it's only the first inning.

The game gets back into motion and our pitcher isn't wasting any time, keeping a fast pace with a mix of strike outs and grounders.

It's the third inning when the battle starts. I grab my hair and twist it, holding it against the back of my head to cool off. I release it and it suddenly has a mind of its own as it flops down onto my scorebooks. I'm sure it's all me, but every time I move or change pencils my hair is there to add complications to my day. Quickly, I tie it up into a knot since I don't have time to dig out my brush for my typical high ponytail. But, by the fourth inning it's falling out and I'm fighting with it again. I'm starting to think I need a scorebook for the battle between me and my hair. I tie it back into a knot and choose which pencil I can do without, stabbing my hair knot with it to keep my hair restrained. Me vs. my hair currently tied at 2.

I'm doing my best to keep focus on the game and not get distracted by Drew in his baseball pants that appear to be tighter than normal. I wonder if he grabbed one of the other players' pants? When I start getting social media messages from friends and colleagues that say congratulations. I ignore them and will respond later, they must be just getting notice that I was honored at the banquet. Anyway, his pants are much tighter across his ass than they usually are though it doesn't seem to be hindering his playing ability. Now that I'm checking him out, his jersey seems big. Maybe we have a new person in charge of uniforms or laundry who needs some help. The jersey has his name and number on it. Could the pants be so tight that they're making the jersey appear bigger? Honestly, it doesn't matter because he'd look gorgeous in a paper sack. Maybe he lost a bet. Oh, or they did that thing where they ask all the players a question and they punked him... "Who wears the tightest pants?" They all answered Brandt and made sure his pants were tight. Hmm, that's a bit elaborate for a group of men.

I gaze down at my scorebooks as soon as I realize I lost a whole inning checking out his pants and find I was on auto-pilot mode, didn't miss a thing.

It's typically the 7th inning when coach pulls the starting pitcher and things get interesting, but not today. Our starting pitcher has been efficient with his pitches and he doesn't pull him until the middle of the 8th when he gives up a 2-run homer. Seals are still ahead by 3, all they need to do is hold them. With 2 outs, coach calls in our closer, the one and only Doug "Super D" Houck, to get 4 outs and give the bull pen a night off. He gets us out of the eighth with one pitch, a pop fly directly to Cross in centerfield.

Bottom of the eighth, Lucine strikes out and Mason draws a walk. Cross is froggy and grounders into a double play.

Top of the ninth, Super D trots out to the mound and starts throwing heat from the get-go. He's ready to get this done and has always pitched well with Seno behind the plate. They strike the first hitter out in three pitches. Second hitter smashes one into the outfield that bounces over the wall in right field, Rock simply couldn't get to it—ground rule double. Third hitter comes up and hits a grounder directly to Brandt for one out and to Martin in time for the double play at first. Seals win and not surprisingly on a double play from the duo of Brandt and Martin, they've been getting at least one in each game and had only one so far. It's all in the statistics.

I need to make notes on this game for my thesis. It's an excellent example of projecting based on player stats.

I review my scorebook and compare it with the scorekeeper, making notes for my future reference. I submit my work for the game and send the coach a message asking what made him change the lineup to the order it was in today. I'm wondering if it was duo driven, but I'm not saying anything about that in my message. I don't want to impact his response in any way.

I pack up my backpack and pull the pencil from my hair to put it away where it belongs. The pencil worked well and didn't take time away from my work. I need to add an extra pencil to my bag just for that purpose, and no need to bring my brush. I put my backpack on and walk out of the press box, grabbing a hot dog on my way through.

"So, does this mean you're not interested in going to happy hour?" A couple of the guys call after me. I shake my head and keep walking. It can't be that big of a difference.

I leave the stadium and walk home with no sign of Drew.

CHAPTER THIRTY-NINE

Drew

I get to the locker room and suddenly there are 5 different phones in my face showing me a video of me dancing with Margaret at the Researching the Sciences banquet. "Who's the chick?" Martin asks looking over my shoulder.

"That's Margaret, the one I was telling you about."

"Did you leave out the part about her being beautiful and how smitten you are?"

I fake chuckle, "I wouldn't say smitten."

Martin takes the phone with the video playing on it out of our teammate's hand and watches it, then shows me, "That's the face of a man who is smitten."

"I told you she's perfect. She ticks all the boxes."

"But, you don't know where to find her."

"There is that." I wish I had her number.

Cross butts in, "I just want to know where you learned to dance like that."

"My high school coach made all the players take dance for a quarter. Originally I thought it was because the dance class was all girls and they didn't have partners to dance with, but it was helpful when he applied what we learned to baseball." Smooth movements, timing, leading without being pushy, working together seamlessly—invaluable. It's probably what gave me the step up to make it to the professional level.

Cross yells across the locker room, "Seno! You want to take dance lessons with me?"

"No!" He shoots back.

Cross walks off grumbling, "You don't have to be a grump. I'm just trying to make us better."

Martin covers his grin, "So how are we finding this chick?"

"Carter is going to see what he can do and I'm going to keep my eye out for her," she'll find me when she's ready.

"Yeah, give it a couple days," Martin nods.

I change into my street clothes and call the pasta restaurant that's on my walk home, ordering my favorite chicken parmigiana with spaghettini, a house green salad, and garlic bread. I hang out in the clubhouse for a few minutes and laughingly offer to show them a couple of the basic dance moves. With no takers, I leave the stadium for my walk home and pick up my dinner on the way.

AFTER DINNER, I wonder if the hoodie girl will be back tonight. Something about her intrigues me regardless of her stalking me or not. I'm the one who presented myself and invited her in.

I turn off everything on the first floor and get comfortable in my bedroom, relaxing in my bed with frequent visits to the window checking for my hoodie girl. Eventually, I give up and I go to bed early.

CHAPTER FORTY

Maggie

I get home to an empty apartment and immediately go to work updating the notes on my thesis and adding today's stats to my projections.

Frank crawls out of the kangaroo pocket of my favorite hoodie and stands on his hind legs staring up at me. I pick him up and hold him to my chest. He climbs up to my shoulder, snuggling into the crook of my neck and my hair. Huh, even Frank likes my hair down.

The apartment door slams, "Mags!" Caroline is instantly in my bedroom doorway and out of breath, "Have you checked your social media?"

"No, I saw some messages popping through during the game but I haven't checked them. I actually forgot about them."

She holds her phone up in front of my face, showing me a video of me dancing with Drew from last night. "You should probably check your messages."

"Who does that? We were at a science department event."

"Along with a whole bunch of other people. You can't do anything without everyone knowing. And it's just going to be worse dating a professional athlete." She grins, "You look fabulous on the dance floor with him."

"Thank you," I reply and check my messages. "He's tagged in all of these posts, but I'm mystery woman?"

"How would they know who you are?"

"I was announced as an honoree last night."

"Apparently people are more interested in the baseball player than science awards."

"What's wrong with people these days. Without science we'd be nowhere."

"I think most people are just happy to pass their science classes and get on with it."

"That's silly. How do you pay bills and budget if you don't understand numbers and statistics? How could you make a decision without knowing the odds?"

"I realize this is crazy, but," she stops and laughs, "Most people make decisions based on what they want and never consider the odds."

"Well that's just frightening."

"Yes, well it's the truth."

I check my messages, "My messages are asking if that's me dancing with Drew Brandt. A couple do congratulate me for being an honoree, but it's more of an afterthought. More of them ask to get Drew to sign a baseball for them." I stare up at Caroline, "Ridiculous!"

"Forget about all of that and check out the way he's looking at you," she zooms in.

"Okay?"

"Can't you see how into you he is?"

"He's such a great dancer."

"That's not the point. Are you so into him that you can't believe he could be into you?"

"Apparently men like me with my hair down."

"Yes, but now that I've seen it for myself—the dress and hair may have caught his eye, but he wants you."

"Then why did he leave without saying goodbye?"

"I don't know."

"Why didn't he ask for my phone number?"

"I don't know."

"Why hasn't he requested my contact information from my alumni file?"

"Most people wouldn't think of that one. It doesn't matter, he's going to see you tomorrow at batting practice and then it will all make sense. Or, if it doesn't at least we will have an answer."

"It was easier watching from the bus shelter with my NVGs," I roll my eyes at her.

"Yes, but now you have the experience of being close to him."

"Whatever. I'm going to bed."

"You mean read?"

"Yep. I'll be by to get coffee in the morning."

"Happy reading," she shakes her head and closes the door behind her.

I close my laptop and lean back into my pillows as I grab my current read. Frank squeals, I tried to squish him again, and grab him to read with me.

I've told myself one more chapter about a dozen times and I need to get to sleep. I set three alarms to be safe and turn the light out.

I'm swept off my feet onto the dance floor by the most gorgeous man. He's tall and light on his feet, it's as if he's floating and taking me with him. His hand is holding mine like a magnet that's meant to be connected, directing me to move at his whim. Twirling me freely around the dance floor as if nobody else exists. He grabs my waist and pulls me to him. His forehead to mine, he stares into my eyes. His hips move against mine as he holds me firm at the small of my back. He claims my lips and runs his hand up my back and neck, threading his fingers through my hair until he's palming the back of my head. Holding me to his desire while his kiss deepens. I'm burning from the inside out with need. He releases me, twirling me again in my desire-filled haze. I reach for him to bring me back in and fulfill my craving, my need to have him take me in his arms and relieve the pain of being mere inches away from him. He wraps his arms around me, kissing my forehead, then my nose, and takes a deep breath as he nuzzles his nose against my cheek, "I need you Maggie."

My alarm goes off abruptly. No, no, no! I slam the snooze button hoping to get back into my dream. Holding my eyes closed. It sounds like Drew, but I can never get a clear view of his face. Finally I got to the kiss, but now it's not enough. The one time the alarm actually wakes me up and I don't fall back asleep! Damn it! I sit up straight in bed and Frank goes flying. I get up and find him climbing my bedspread to get back on the bed, and give him a helping hand back to a comfortable nesting spot.

I need coffee and wonder if I'm allowed to wear my hoodie to the coffee stand, it defeats the purpose if I have to be ready for public viewing.

Me: Am I allowed to wear my big hoodie to pick up my coffee?
Caroline: Sure, but I don't know why you'd want to.
Caroline: Remember the attention you got yesterday?
Caroline: Plus it's a warm morning.
Me: Can I just put my hoodie on and pick up my coffee?
Caroline: I'll make it for you right now.

Yay! I pull my oversized hoodie on over my leggings, grab my keys, slide into my sneakers, and I'm out the door. Hood up, so I don't even have to do my hair. It's the little things. I just need coffee. Halfway to the coffee stand I put my hands in my kangaroo pocket and find out I'm not alone, Frank is hitchhiking along on this excursion. I need to remember to check on that when I put my hoodie on if it's been where he can get to it. I rub his little belly in my pocket to keep tabs on him and make sure I don't lose him somewhere on the way.

I walk up to the coffee stand and find Caroline in her neon pink eighties workout finery, "Good morning."

"It speaks," she says. "What is this non-determinable blob before me?" She hands me a large coffee.

"Ha ha. Thank you." I keep one hand on Frank in my pocket and delight at the hot elixir I sip on.

"At least I don't have to worry about anybody hitting on you on your walk home," she calls after me and I just keep walking.

CHAPTER FORTY-ONE

Drew

I walk up to the coffee stand happy to find the lively girl with the pink headband, "Good morning."

She turns around and seems surprised, "Good morning, what can I get for you today?"

"Large coffee please," oh, and do you have any information on the adorable hoodie girl you can share with me? I can't ask that. She did say it's her roommate.

"Anything else,?" She asks.

"Can you help me out? When would be a good time to run into your roommate picking up her coffee?" I stop embarrassed. "Sorry, I shouldn't have asked."

She looks down the street and stretches up onto her tiptoes trying to lean over the counter, "You just missed her."

I let out a nervous chuckle, "Well, maybe next time."

She nods at me and gets to making my coffee. "You sure you don't want a smoothie this morning?" She calls back over her shoulder.

"No, it's definitely a coffee day and you make the best coffee."

"You can go ahead and pay on the notepad," she says.

I take care of my payment and she has my coffee ready for me before I'm done, "I hope you don't mind, I had a new stencil I wanted to try."

I grab my coffee to check it out thinking anything will ruin it. Her coffee is already perfect. I find a light dusting of powdered sugar in the shape of a baseball with the stitching in the negative space. "Thank you. That's fun."

"Give it a try and let me know if it's too sweet. I tried to balance it."

I sip the coffee and get a sweet hit, then it's perfect again. "It's got a hit of sweetness upfront, but then it's perfect," I smile at her.

"Maybe tomorrow we can try it with a cocoa and powdered sugar mix," she grins.

"I'm in. Have a great day," I drop a $10 in her tips jar and wander off the way she looked for her roommate. I have no idea why. She's so far ahead of me, I won't find her. I'm not sure why I care enough to even ask about her. Margaret will find me and she's perfect. I suppose I'm curious about the big hoodie. Is there a big hoodie club around here? Maybe she's friends with the big hoodie that has the NVGs? Or I suppose it could be her. Why had I never considered that before? I should ask the coffee girl if her roommate owns night vision goggles—she'd think I'm crazy.

I find myself heading toward the stadium, so I go in early for a workout. On my way into the locker room Carter pulls me into his office, "Close the door behind you please."

"No problem," I close the door and wait for more.

"So I asked around a bit and the Seals have an employee

with the name M. M. Hamilton. I don't know if that helps or not, but it's a start," he says.

"Do we know anything else about them? Is the person female? What's their job title? Anything?" I ask hoping for something to find out if we're on the right track.

"My contact referred to her as a she. I was trying not to break privacy guidelines so I didn't push."

"It's something. All employees have ID badges, right?"

"Yes."

"Are there photos and names somewhere accessible?" I ask hopeful. "Or even the position she works in?"

"I'll see what else I can find out, but I wanted to let you know where we are so far."

"Thank you," I get up to leave.

"Oh, one more thing."

"Yea?"

"I reached out to your mother. She's a very sweet woman who made it extremely clear that she didn't belong at your place of work, and she offered to make me a lasagna," he laughs.

"I hope you took her up on the lasagna. Best you'll ever eat."

"I'll remember that for next time. I've got something else I'm going to try," he grins and dismisses me.

I'm hopeful that I'll run into Margaret, but I didn't think it was so bad that I'd start hallucinating. I swear the woman sitting in the stands just off first base is her spitting image, if there's anyone sitting there at all. It makes sense that she'd work for the team in some capacity, but wouldn't she have mentioned that to me? I guess we didn't get to talk much and it was hard to hear with the music and crowd. I didn't manage to get her number, so we didn't get far. I glance in her direction and wink at her from my position at second base. I must be losing it. Who winks? She smiles the most beautiful smile in return. I'm observing as the pitching coach throws batting practice and occasionally picking the ball when it gets close. Martin and I have been studying pitches and my position is probably the best place for it. She's content sitting there alone watching batting practice with her long dark hair cascading over her shoulders and her feet up on the seat in front of her showing me her long tan legs.

Martin whistles at me, and I nod at him, "Where's your head?"

I grab my cock and lift my chin toward Margaret without thinking. I hope she didn't notice that. I'm not the guy that's after sex. I want more. I want her in my arms, in my house, in my life, drinking coffee with me, and everything that goes with it.

Martin stares back at me with big eyes, and mouths, "Is that her?"

I nod with his assurance that there's actually someone there.

At least I'm not imagining her. She's focused on batting practice like she's a scout. It's time to switch to hitting, so I take the long way to the backstop and walk straight toward her instead of cutting across the diamond. I stop right in from of her and look at her long and hard to make sure I'm not losing it. But I don't have any words and all I can do is drool. I turn and walk to the backstop, frustrated with myself.

Martin walks up behind me, "Good job, Cassanova."

"What do you expect me to do out here at batting practice?"

"Get the girl. I don't care where you are."

I stand behind the backstop spinning my bat anxiously considering how to get the girl.

Seno standing in earshot leans my way, "Impress her with your bat. It's cheesy, but it works."

Cross adds on, "Always listen to Seno."

Mason chimes in with, "Yup, or Sherry. They know shit."

I swing the bat around as I walk into the batting cage and gaze at her while I put my helmet on. She turns around like she's searching for something, but there's nothing there besides her and a couple of the guys from the press.

Okay, pay attention. I swing at the first pitch, hitting a grounder up the middle. That's not impressive. I hit the next one down the foul line into left field, which is skill but still not impressive.

Seno from behind the backstop, "Wait for the right pitch and do it right."

I let the next two pitches go by. I face her direction, obviously staring at her and point at her.

"I like the drama, now back it up," Seno comments.

It's my perfect pitch and I swing with everything I've got. The crack off my bat tells me it's out of the park and I watch as it sails out into the left field grandstands.

"Close the deal, baby!" Martin yells.

I walk out of the batting cage with purpose, throwing my bat and helmet to the dugout. I walk up to her and wish there wasn't a net separating us. I take off my sunglasses, "Margaret? Right?" Don't let me have the wrong woman. I don't have to wait for her response, her eyes tell me everything I need.

She nods, "I go by Maggie now."

"I like that. Why don't I see you at batting practice more often?"

"It's not part of my job."

She is M. M. Hamilton! "Why today?"

"Sometimes I need baseball to be fun, not work," she smiles and my whole body heats up.

"I get that. Maybe we can go to the batting cages sometime and have some fun," I need to think before I speak. I already asked her to coffee and she vanished.

"I've never been."

"You'll love it," I lean into the net and she stands, moving in closer.

"I'm in," she says gazing up at me, but it's like she's in for more than the batting cages and I take her queue.

Her hands meet mine on the net. I lick my lips and she moves in closer. I lean into the net, my fingers reaching through to caress her face and our lips meet. She's soft and sweet, and into this kiss as much as I am. She pushes on the net, so she can reach me and grabs my shirt, twisting it with her fingers. The team hoots and hollers, and the spell is broken. We both step back from the net and she's all of a sudden shy with her hands stuffed in her back pockets.

"May I have your number? I've been kicking myself for not getting it from you the other night," I wait for her to respond.

She passes me her phone through the net, "You don't have your phone at batting practice, send yourself a text." She smiles as I do as she suggests.

I hand back her phone, "Please don't disappear this time." I smile at her and force myself to get back to practice.

I LOOK for Maggie when batting practice is over, but she's already gone. I get to my locker and send her a text:

Me: Hi.

Me: I have so many questions for you.

Me: Most important first, what time are you off work tonight?

Me: What's your position here?

Why isn't she answering? I need to chill out, but I just got her back. She's probably working.

Maggie: I'm done with work 20 to 30 minutes after the game is over.

Maggie: I'm the team statistician. I sit near the score-keeper in the press box.

Me: Of course you are!

Me: I'll look for you when I go back out on the field.

Is it too soon?

Me: Can I see you after the game?

CHAPTER FORTY-TWO

Maggie

> Me: He kissed me!
> Me: Now he's texting me.
> Caroline: Why are you texting me? Text him!
> Me: He wants to see me after the game.
> Me: What do I do?
> Caroline: How was the kiss?
> Caroline: Do you want to see him after the game?
> Me: Yes.
> Caroline: Tell him!
> Me: But he's going to figure it out. We both live close and I know where he lives.
> Caroline: How was the kiss?
> Me: Perfect. Amazing. Chemical.

Chemical? The piece I've been waiting for. We have chemistry.

I text Drew:

Me: Tonight would be great.
Me: Where should I meet you?
Drew: Wait for me in the Press Box?
Me: Okay.
Me: Where are we going?
Drew: Wherever you want, but I don't have my car here with me.
Me: I don't have my car either.
Drew: How are you getting home?
Me: I walk.
Drew: Me, too. Maybe we can go someplace local and I can walk you home?
Me: Perfect.

I sit quiet and still in my chair, absorbing the afternoon and everything that goes with it. On the inside I'm screaming at the top of my lungs. I've been waiting for him to kiss me for so long. The kiss is everything. In my heart he's been the one for as long as I can remember, but the chemistry we have? I had no idea what to expect or if I'd recognize it when it happened. It was more exciting than a home run. I'd liken it to being on a coffee IV with the straight hit of caffeine directly to my system. I couldn't breathe, yet I could finally breathe at the same time. All of my wires were crossed and confused. The only thing that was for sure? Us.

Unless. What if he didn't get any of the same reaction I did and I'm simply a crazy girl who's had a crush on him for way too long? It's hard to determine. I don't have much to compare it to. I've always compared every guy to Drew and, well, that doesn't work out so well for every other man on the face of the earth. And, of course, apparently I've been invisible in my hoodie which limited my suitors. So, for the record, an over-sized hoodie is like camouflage and men like women to wear their hair down. I was comfy and happy in my hoodie, nothing is as comforting as a huge hoodie you can get lost in. Though I'm willing to let Drew test it and find a way to be my favorite thing to get lost in. I wonder if the chemistry gets more intense?

I turn on the pregame to get my head in the game while I get my pencils and scorebooks out.

The scorekeeper turns to me, "Did you change your hair or something? You look so different the last couple days. In a good way."

"You're just used to me wearing my hoodie and having my hair in a ponytail. I changed it up a little," I reply.

"Huh, well whatever you did works for you," he nods.

"Thank you."

I turn back to my work and find Drew standing in the middle of the infield waving at me. I wave back and my cheeks get warm. I watch as he gets the biggest grin before disappearing back into the dugout.

I text Caroline:

Me: I'm going to be late tonight.

Me: Don't wait up for me.

Caroline: That's fine. I'll check your location on my phone to make sure you're safe.

Me: Thanks for looking out for me.

Caroline: It's a horrible job, but somebody's got to do it. 😒

Caroline: Does this mean you're going to show him your hoohaw?

Me: I'm not planning on it.

Me: Though, it did occur to me that it could be the only opportunity.

Caroline: I'm going to need you to elaborate.

Me: When he figures out I'm the stalker he might not be interested anymore.

Me: So, is it one of those things where I do it when I have the option or I'll regret it and wonder for the rest of my life?

Caroline: Interesting.

Caroline: What's the odds on morals vs regrets?

Me: On a timeline I believe regretting it would be worse. The "what if" question would never go away.

Me: However, if a pregnancy occurs, morals would stick with me for just as long and have a bigger impact on the remainder of my life in a multitude of ways.

Caroline: But what are the chances that you get pregnant?

Me: Condoms are 98% effective, but that doesn't include human error, and they break up to 12% of the time depending on the brand.

Caroline: What are the odds of a professional baseball player using a condom?

Me: I don't think there are any studies on that. I would guess the more sex they have, the more likely they are to use condoms to avoid STDs. But that might be too logical of an assumption for the control group we're talking about.

Me: What's with all the questions? Are you poking fun at my statistical nature?

Caroline: 🤭

Me: Game is going to start.

Caroline: Wait!

Caroline: What did you decide? Morals or regrets?

Me: Regrets. But I don't think it will happen tonight.
Caroline: Have fun on your date.

I focus on the game. Damn he's gorgeous. The way he moves with fluid motion. Okay, stats and scorekeeping could be a challenge tonight.

The game was an interesting one. The most important thing is that the Seals won, but none of the challenges went the way they appeared to me or the scorekeeper. We both glared at each other when the teams challenged, unsure what they were trying to accomplish when the play appeared to be clean and obvious. Personally, I think the Seals coach started challenging calls simply to get back at the other team. There is a line somewhere between challenge and just let it go and play the game, unfortunately the opposing coach is apparently not privy to said line. Or he could just be an asshole. I wonder if he has to challenge everything he can to try to make up for how crappy his team is? It would be horrible to feel like that. Honestly, new rules are always a problem. People overall don't understand the intricacies of them, and that includes some of the players and coaches. And the challenges themselves? None of them were anything I anticipated them being. All of them were a contributing component of the play, not anything direct with the ball and the hitter. The strangeness of the game led the scorekeeper and I to take time to review how we scored them and how I noted the stats. Important to verify accuracy of things that aren't clear.

I'm taking longer than normal to review my data before I submit it, but that's just the way it is. None of it is any good if it's not correct. I pull the pencil from my hair and gather my pencils back into their pouch. I get all my stuff packed into my backpack and sit watching the grounds crew while I wait for Drew.

CHAPTER FORTY-THREE

Drew

The game was weird, and I'm letting it go to move on to the rest of my evening. I shower and change into my street clothes in record time.

Martin glances over at me, "Going somewhere?"

"Yep."

"The woman?"

"Yes, and her name is Maggie. She's not a secret."

"What's the plan?"

"No plan. Just going to spend some time with her."

"Have fun," he fist bumps me.

I get out of the locker room, walk through the tunnel to the stadium center elevator, and take it up to the media level. I exit the elevator and go left walking through the press box concessions area and stop on the top step of the press box. It's a beautiful view of the field, calm and serene. Nobody is left except Maggie sitting at her desk in the front left corner with her Air Pods in, tapping her toes and bouncing her head. She pulls her knees up to her chest and spins in her chair, about falling out of her chair when she's startled by my presence and trying to get her dignity back. She doesn't need to, I love her young exuberance.

I smile and walk to her, "Hi." I take her hand and pull her out of her chair. Leaning in to give her a kiss without missing a beat. Her lips are exactly how I left them, sweet and soft. And I want more of them. I wrap my arms around her and my body relaxes for the first time in weeks. Something about her makes me want to take care of her, simply hold her.

She reaches her hands up around the back of my neck and gazes up at me, "Hi." She twirls the hair at the nape of my neck in her fingers. I don't need anything more.

"Would you like to get something to eat or a drink?" I ask trying to give us direction when I'm happy to stay right where I am and not say a single word.

"Let's get out of the stadium," her eyes sparkle waiting for approval of her suggestion.

I nod and she grabs her backpack to put it on, "Let me carry that for you." I take it from her and sling it over one shoulder. Taking her hand as we walk to the elevator, she leads the way out. We exit through the employee gate into the village. "Which way do you walk home?" I ask.

"I walk up here, then I take a right, and walk six or seven more blocks. You don't have to walk me home," she replies.

"I walk the same direction, but not as far," I say. "I moved in a couple months ago after having the house refurbished and updated. My great grandfather had it built and did quite a bit of the work on it himself."

"It's amazing that your home has always been owned by the Brandt family. So much history."

"I spent a lot of time there when I was a kid, lots of happy memories. Though it wasn't originally the Brandt family, the house is from my mother's side. I suppose I should put up a sign that says 'Bellisario.'" There's music coming from somewhere, getting louder as we walk. "It's convenient for me with the stadium so close. What brought you here?"

"My dorm mate. When she had to get out of the dorms, she moved in with her long-time best friend. They found a place and she moved. But the best friend ghosted her. I've been her roommate ever since. The location is perfect for both of us since she works right around the corner, and I walk to the stadium and do most of my thesis work remotely."

The music continues to get louder, it's coming from one of the rooftops. I stop and drop her backpack on the sidewalk, never letting go of her hand. I pull her to me and dance. The volume gets turned up as we dance to "Parallel Line," by Keith Urban. So fitting. I always wondered how couples found their song, but it seems the song finds you. I hold her close, occasionally leading her to a slow twirl. Just us under the stars and the street lights, turning into more of a sway as we meld together and tenderly claim each other's lips.

CHAPTER FORTY-FOUR

Maggie

We walk up to my building and I don't want the evening to end. If this is a dream, I don't want to wake up. He's held my hand in his all evening without letting go. I don't want him to let go and I squeeze his hand. "This is my building."

"Can I see you again tomorrow?" He stares at the ground. "We talked about so many things, but I still want to hear about your thesis. Sounds like it might be a discussion that requires sitting and coffee," he grins. "I've been distracted by your lips tonight." He leans in and gives me a quick sweet kiss.

"I'd love that."

"Perfect, plan on having dinner with me tomorrow night. I'll meet you in the press box and we can walk home together."

"That works for me." I turn to go and then back to him, "Goodnight."

He doesn't release my hand, "May I walk you to your door?"

I smile and nod. I lead him up the half flight of stairs to my door at the end of the hall on the left, "This is me." I notice the lights are still on through the peephole and suddenly it's dark. Suspicious.

"Will you be at batting practice tomorrow?"

"I'm almost always there for batting practice, you just don't see me."

"I see you now," he gazes deep into my eyes and places his hands on my cheeks, holding me where he wants me as he presses his lips to mine with a commanding need. Again I find myself burning from the inside out with desire for this man. Should I invite him in? Should I whisper in his ear, offering him my body? Should I simply hold on and never let go? Should I drop to my knees right here and give him a blow job (I'd have to learn how real quick)? I hold my body tighter against him. The kiss intensifies, pressing me against my door while his right hand grips my hair holding it tight and his left holds me by the small of my back. He pulls away breathing heavily, "I see you now." He scrubs his hand over his face, "I'll see you tomorrow. Goodnight." He turns and walks away quickly. I stand there for a moment absorbing everything and finding that I want more.

The door that's holding me up moves behind me, "Are you coming in or staying outside all night?"

"Were you watching?" I ask Caroline.

"Nooooooo. I would never do that," she grins.

"I saw the light through the peephole and then it was blocked," I tap my foot.

"What do you think? If your roommate was dating potentially the most eligible bachelor on the Seals would you be watching?" She stares at me with big eyes awaiting a response.

"But my roommate isn't dating a Seal, I am!"

"Yes you are and he's hot. Geez! That kiss looked mind-blowing."

"That man makes me wish I was more experienced. I wanted to drop down to my knees and suck his cock."

"Trust me, they aren't that picky. You'll be fine. Don't be afraid of it."

"Noted."

"Tell me everything or at least the highlights," Caroline follows me into my bedroom and sits on the foot of my bed.

"Besides the goodnight kiss that you witnessed, he held my hand and we walked around the village and talked. The rooftop bar was playing music so he grabbed me and danced with me on the sidewalk below it until he couldn't help but kiss me. It was super romantic."

"Did he do that kind of pull your hair thing at the door?"

"Yea."

"What did you think of that?"

"At first I was wondering what the hell but then I wanted more."

"He wouldn't have done it if your hair was up in a ponytail."

"Understood."

"Anything else?"

"Same thing tomorrow night and I'm having dinner with him."

"Maybe take something to change into that doesn't say Seals on it for dinner?"

"Maybe just a different shirt to change into with my jeans?"

"That would work. A cute dress would be nice too."

"Don't push it."

"Think about it. Could be comfortable with some leggings under it or some tights. Definitely sexier."

I roll my eyes, "I have to go to bed so I can dream about Drew."

"What's new about that?" She asks from my doorway.

"I'm not reading a romance, I'm in it."

CHAPTER FORTY-FIVE

Drew

I wake up well-rested and looking forward to my date with Maggie. I lay in bed and download the song we danced to last night and find myself making a playlist. I call my mom...

"Hello?"

"Hi, mom."

"Good morning, dear."

"I just want to tell you I went on a date last night before you get news from somewhere else."

"Is it the girl you were dancing with at the banquet?"

"How do you know about that?"

"Honey, it was all over the internet. I follow you all over social media, but I prefer the reels on Insta. You're a wonderful dancer."

"Yes, it's her. I'm having dinner with her for the first time tomorrow."

"I'll make a lasagna and leave it in your oven. She's not a vegetarian or anything like that is she?"

"No, mom."

"You know I took a couple screen shots when I could see her face and zoomed in, I'm old and I can't see the little stuff so well. Anyway, is she the girl that was your scorekeeper in high school?"

"Why did I call you? You already know everything."

"You're busy. I have to keep up somehow."

"Okay, love you mom."

"Love you too, dear."

I hang up and a text pops through at the same time.

Martin: Long run this morning?

Me: I'm not out of bed yet.

Martin: Don't let me interrupt your in-bed activities 😎

Me: Not like that. Late night and I finally got some sleep.

Martin: My way was more fun.

Me: Probably soon.

Me: Give me an hour and I'll be ready for the run.

Martin: You got it. I'll pick you up. Be ready to run.

Me: 👍

I wonder if...

Me: Good Morning.

Me: I had a great time last night.

Me: Can't wait to kiss you again.

I don't think she's a morning person, but when she wakes up my messages will be there. I close my eyes for a couple of minutes and remember what it's like to hold her and kiss her. I may have gone too far at her door last night, but she was driving me crazy. I want more of her. I want all of her. Fuck me, I want inside her.

We pull into the player's garage after our run along Shelter Island, prepared to spend some time in the workout room.

Carter grabs me as I walk by his office. "I plead the fifth as to how I got this," he says and shows me her employee ID photo.

"Thank you. I appreciate your efforts. We went on our first date last night. It's all good."

"So you don't need this anymore?"

"It's actually very helpful and confirms something for me that I'd been wondering about," I nod.

"Are you going to share?"

I close the door to Carter's office, "M. M. Hamilton is the woman I danced with at the banquet, the woman I kissed at batting practice yesterday, our team statistician, the adorable hoodie girl I've been wondering about at the coffee stand, and the owner of a pair of night vision goggles."

"She's the beauty and the stalker?"

"Yes."

"Anything else we need to know about her?"

"Yeah, she's mine and I'm keeping her."

"Then I guess I don't need to ask the next question."

"What was that?"

"Do I need to have her fired or reported for stalking."

"No. Not necessary. But thank you for taking care of all of us on the team. We truly appreciate it and I don't think we say it enough."

"Of course."

I walk into the workout room expecting to find only

Martin there waiting for me to spot him, "Well, it's confirmed."

"What?" Asks Cross.

I check the room and it's full of everybody except Martin. "Nothing."

"Oh, it was something. That tone, definitely something about the woman," Cross nods.

"I have to agree," Seno adds from the bench he's lifting on.

"You gave it away in your step," Houck added. "Not just a woman. It's a woman you want to keep."

"Yeah, totally a woman," Mason chimes in. "I mean, Seno is always right about this stuff."

Martin walks in and surveys the room, "What did I miss?"

"Brandt here said it's confirmed and we figure it's something about the woman. It's always a woman," Mason takes control as if he wasn't just going along with the others.

"Confirmed, huh?" Martin stares at Brandt and laughs.

"Yep."

"What gave it away?" Martin asks trying not to share all of my personal business.

"The hoodie."

"Didn't you say there are two hoodie girls?"

"Yep. She's both."

"Hold on. Hold on," Cross says as he takes the floor. "Is that gorgeous woman you were kissing at batting practice yesterday also your stalker?"

I hang my head, and Martin adds, "He spent the evening with her last night, too."

"Hey, I like her. She's not really a stalker. She makes me happy. And she doesn't know that I'm aware of her watching me with her night vision goggles. Though she has to know that I think somebody was watching me."

"Why is that?" Houck asks.

"I don't want to get into that," I shut my mouth.

"Probably best," Martin laughs.

Carter pops his head in, "Look, she's an extremely intelligent young lady and our team statistician. Not a stalker. You all need to let it go."

"Hey Carter," Seno butts in. "Can you send that woman a Brandt jersey up to her desk please?"

"Of course," Carter nods like he was expecting that.

Martin chimes in, "Hey Carter, can you send her an oversized hoodie with Brandt on it, too? The biggest one you've got."

"Sure," he shakes his head. "Drew, you want to add to the list?"

I shake my head, "I think they've got it covered."

Carter nods and gets out before they come up with more work for him.

I stare at Martin, "I didn't want to have to discuss the stalker thing with her. I was just going to let it go like it didn't happen.

"So?" Martin jests.

"So, that's pointing right at it. That's how I know it's her. She always wore an oversized hoodie and now that I think about it, that's why she doesn't wear them anymore. She's trying not to get caught," I hang my head.

"Or maybe it's not hoodie weather?" Mason offers.

Martin points at Mason, "He has a point. It might not be hoodie weather. You're always overthinking everything."

"None of it matters. She's smart and he likes her, that's what's important. Support your teammate," Seno barks. "Also, never fuck with someone who can screw with your stats. I'm not saying she would, but that's just common sense." They all nod in agreement and my phone starts dinging with texts.

Maggie: Hi.
Maggie: I thought last night was a dream.
Maggie: Waking up to your texts proved it was real.

Martin glares at me, "What now smiley?"

"Uh, I'm going to walk the warning track," I say and leave the room to the sound of my teammates making kissing noises. Whatever. They've all been in my position.

I get past first base on the warning track and dial Maggie. "Drew?"

"Good morning sunshine," I say shocked by the sweetness in my own voice.

She yawns, "I'm not completely awake yet. Caffeine deficiency." She giggles and I get hard. Fuck me.

"I slept well last night, and woke up thinking about you."

"Where are you now?"

"Walking the warning track. Where are you?"

"I'm in my bed, snuggled down into my blankets."

Is it too soon to tell her I wish I was there with her? Or actually, that I wish she was in my bed when I woke up this morning. I definitely wouldn't have managed to go run with Martin. "Sounds warm and cozy."

"It is. And it's quiet because my roommate works mornings."

Right, at the coffee stand I think to myself, "My house is always quiet. It's too big for just me."

"You'll grow into it. Give it a chance, you haven't been there long."

"You think?"

"Yeah. All the house and neighborhood sounds will become familiar. It's your family house. It's perfect for you."

I think you're perfect for me, "You're probably right. It's just not how I remember it. I was never there alone. It was always the whole family with all the kids running around, and my mom and nonna in the kitchen making something that smelled delectable."

"Have some friends or family over, make it feel like home."

"I'm starting with having you over. Dinner at my place tonight. Is that okay?"

"I can't think of anything more perfect," her smile shines through in her voice.

"Okay, then I'll see you tonight."

She giggles, "I'll be watching you at batting practice."

Apparently she likes watching me, "Are you at the stadium to watch every batting practice?"

"Most, but not all. It's not part of my job, but observing batting practice has helped me with my research. Insight into what the players are working on and their relationships with their teammates."

"We need time to talk baseball and your thesis. It may need to wait until the offseason to have enough time for that one," I chuckle.

"It's true. Time is limited."

"Me, too. I need to finish my workout. See you tonight," I hang up.

CHAPTER FORTY-SIX

Maggie

So far today is fabulous. Waking up to messages from the man of my dreams, unprecedented. Never in my wildest imagination did I think that would happen. Yet here I am concerned that I don't have enough time to get my numbers updated, get ready for work and a date, and get to the stadium in time for batting practice. I need time to do my hair, which I don't typically allow for. Do I take clothes to change into after the game? Are my work clothes acceptable for dinner at his house? I'm going in his house. Is he cooking? I hope he doesn't expect me to cook. Should I be taking anything to contribute? A host gift? I remember somebody telling me to never go to someone's house empty-handed. I need Caroline.

Me: Good morning.
Caroline: Good afternoon, but okay.
Me: I don't have time to pick up coffee today.

Caroline: Do you have a fever?

Me: Seriously, I have too much to do.

Me: I need your assistance.

Caroline: Shoot.

Me: Dinner at his house tonight.

Caroline: That sounds nice.

Me: Do I take clothes to change into after the game or just wear my work clothes?

Caroline: That depends. Are you going to be cuddling on the couch or staying over?

Me: Don't make it worse. I'm already starting to freak out over it.

Caroline: You don't have to wear Seals gear every time you go to work. Dress for your date.

Me: I have to wear my Seals shirt. I've worn a team shirt to every game I've kept score or statistics at since junior high.

Caroline: You can miss once.

Me: Nope. If I don't wear my Seals shirt and they lose, it could be my fault.

Caroline: There's no logic in that statement. I'd take a shirt to change. He doesn't want to be thinking about baseball when he's with you.

Me: How do you know what he wants to think about when he's with me? What if he gets bored with me?

Caroline: He's a man. If he's alone with you and thinking about baseball it's because you brought up your thesis or he's trying to keep from getting a hard-on.

Me: That's offensive.

Caroline: It's the truth. And you should be taking that as a compliment.

Me: I suppose.

Caroline: Take that soft slinky feeling tunic length top you

have and your nicest leggings. I'd tell you not to wear
your sneakers, but you're walking to work and back.
Me: I can do that.
Me: Why leggings and the soft shirt?
Caroline: Do you want his hands on you?
Me: Got it.
Me: Should I be taking something with me? Host gift?
Caroline: No. It's just you and him. Let him be in charge.
Me: He hasn't been there long and I was thinking of
maybe a house warming gift.
Caroline: Maybe, but after you've been there a couple
times then you can consider that.
Me: Fair. Okay, I have to get ready.
Caroline: Wear sexy panties and a bra that matches.
Nothing grandma-ish.
Caroline: Does tonight count as the third date?
Me: Second date.
Caroline: Anything else?
Me: If you're going to be home in time, will you please
bring me coffee?
Caroline: We'll see.

I have less time than I thought. I'll be working on my
updates during batting practice, but at least I can do it from
my desk in the press box.

First things first, I dump my underwear drawer out on my
bed and toss anything even the slightest bit grandma-ish back
into the drawer. I lay out all the bras and go through the
panties one by one in hopes of finding something that's sexy
and matches. Sexy has never been my goal when it comes to
bras and panties. Comfortable, cheap, cotton—these are the
things I want, but not today. Maybe they overlap with sexy
somewhere in this mess. I envision my bed as a Venn diagram

and start moving the pieces around. Panties on the left, bras on the right, matching where they overlap, and an almost non-existent sexy stuff on the top. I don't have many options and I have no time to go shopping. The choice is pink polka dots or black and I go with black so my leggings aren't accidentally see-thru to polka dots. Black lace thong and, magically, the matching black lace bra. Caroline must have bought the set for me as a gift. I leave them out together on the top of my dresser and hit the shower. It's a full-on shower day, hair wash and condition, shave my legs and my armpits, exfoliate with body scrub—the works. I can't risk getting close and having legs like a lumberjack. At least my fingernails and toenails are still polished from my banquet prep.

I tie my wet hair up in a towel, step into my sexy panties, and get my bra fastened in place. I toss the clothes I need to change into in my backpack, pull on my jeans, and a Seals shirt. I blow dry my hair with my round brush and give my ends a little bit of a flip. I swipe some mascara on and I'm good to go. I double check my backpack to make sure I have everything and slide into my shoes, ready to walk to the door and grab a hot dog when I get to the stadium.

When I realize I didn't see Frank this morning. I go back to my bedroom and check his usual places, everywhere around my pillow, under the blankets, no Frank. I consider closing my blackout drapes and powering up my NVGs to find him. But I hear a quiet scratching in my dresser and find him in my underwear drawer. You don't suppose I emptied the drawer onto him and tossed him back in like he was granny panties? Did he climb in? Or was he already in there? It doesn't matter. I found him. I give him a hug and a peck on the head, then place him on my pillow with the blanket scrunched up around him.

I head out the door, running behind now with the Frank

search and pass Caroline coming into the building. She hands me an extra-large coffee as we pass each other without stopping. "Thank you. You're a goddess!" I call over my shoulder to her.

"You're welcome. Have fun and get some," she yells at me in response.

I pick up my pace and try to get to the stadium before batting practice starts.

I'm never this late and now there's a line at the employee gate to get in. I hear balls cracking against bats in the background. I hate not being ready when batting practice starts, it's all part of my process.

I get to my desk in time to watch the last couple hitters take their at bats and all the Seals walk off the field. It's probably a good thing, I don't want to be a distraction for Drew. I need to journal our dates and monitor if anything impacts his playing, just for my information of course. I set up my workspace and put my Air Pods on to listen to the pregame. I'm ready to update my numbers, but I'm starving so I grab a hot dog and a soda before I get to work.

I'm startled by a tap on my shoulder and find a bald man holding a jersey and a huge oversized hoodie, "Ms. Hamilton?"

I stare at him unsure, "Yes."

He nods, "I was asked to get these to you."

"Thank you," I take the two items from him and he disappears. I stop to look them over. A missy jersey in my size with Brandt and his number 29 on the back and one of the hoodies the players wear in a huge size also with is name and number on the back.

I immediately put the jersey on over my Seals shirt and text him.

Me: Thank you for the jersey and the hoodie.
Drew: You're welcome.
Drew: I didn't see you at batting practice.
Me: I was running late today.
Drew: I've been thinking about you all day.
Me: Me?
Drew: Yes, you.
Drew: See you in a few hours.

I spin giddily and get back to updating my numbers for my thesis.

The team runs out onto the field and Drew gazes up at me and smiles when he gets into position.

Time to go to work for both of us.

There's nothing extraordinary about the game and that's a good thing because all I can focus on is being naked with Drew. I manage to keep score and maintain stats, only double checking with the scorekeeper twice. Seals win 2-1. It would've kept my attention if there was more action, but the teams were both efficient with a game time of only two hours and fourteen minutes. I've been keeping track of the game times as a side note. More stats, more accuracy.

I go through my postgame routine and submit the game statistics. Watching the time carefully, I dig my change of clothes out of my backpack and run up to the ladies' room to change. The easy change gives me a dressier, more feminine vibe. I fold my jersey up neatly and pack it into my backpack. The hoodie is super bulky, I stare at it and my backpack thinking you can't fit 2 cups into a 1 cup container, and leave it to sit while I focus on inputting my numbers and I wait for Drew.

Drew: On my way.

I finish up quickly and save my work. I slide my laptop into the laptop sleeve of my backpack and wind up my cord to go with it. I get all of my pencils in their pouch and stowed, and squeeze my scorebooks in with my laptop in an attempt to make the most room possible for the hoodie. It's different than my hoodie. It's thick, more formed and stiffer, and I can't just shove it in and make it fit. Obviously a man's hoodie, it even has a pull cord down around the waist. I'm standing here staring at it when this hot baseball player steps into the doorway of the press box and stands there rocking back and forth on his feet with his hands in the front pockets of his jeans. His hair curling at the edges with a mind of its own. The blue button-up he's wearing makes his eyes shine even brighter, tucked in with the top buttons undone.

"Hey beautiful," his deep voice rolls through me and exposes my vulnerabilities. "You look nice tonight."

I grin like a child, "You too."

He walks toward me and picks up the hoodie, chuckling, "This isn't from me. The guys did this, well Martin mostly." He stops uncertainty in his tone, "That's the largest one I've seen. Was it bigger than Carter when he delivered it?"

"Picking on me? Why would they do that? I haven't even met them."

"First, you're beautiful and fun and we support each other as teammates."

"Fun?"

"Definitely."

"How's that?"

"Do I really need to explain the second part?"

He kisses me, shooting a powerful energy through my body and making me weak at the knees. I nod.

"Okay." He takes a deep breath. He makes sure his arms are wrapped around me tightly and holds me close, "Second, you're the adorable hoodie girl and I've been wondering why you own a pair of night vision goggles."

My cheeks get warm and I'm 100% positive I'm bright red. Tears build in my eyes and my ears start ringing. Why is he still holding onto me? He said it. It's over.

I turn my head so he can't see my embarrassment and pull away from him, but he doesn't let go, "Where are you going?"

"Somewhere far away from you so you don't have me arrested and place a restraining order on me that will make me have to move and give Caroline the right to say 'I told you so.'" He chuckles and it infuriates me. "Let me go!"

"Is that what you want? Because I don't want to let you go. I want to keep you right here in my arms and take you home with me."

"What?"

"Something about you. You're everything I was searching for and so much more. You keep me on my toes. Maybe you can teach me some surveillance techniques," he grins.

"You don't think I'm a stalker?" I probably shouldn't use that word.

"I understand where someone might think that, but no."

"Oh no! So, the team knows about my NVGs?" I cover my face.

"I only told Martin, you can blame him for that one."

I squint my eyes, "Is he still here?"

"Probably. You want to meet him?"

"Yes I do." I grab the hoodie and pull it on over my head. It's like being swallowed by a whale. It hangs down to my knees and I could probably fit two more of me in here.

Drew chuckles, "It's like a dress, all you need is a belt to give it some shape."

He takes my hand and I'm flooded with relief. There's no

more secrets. He's still holding my hand. He sends a text and takes the lead. We get out of the elevator at the tunnel and his phone dings, "Good... I have approval."

"What do we need approval for?"

"Don't worry about it. We're almost there."

We walk up to the door of the team locker room, he opens the door and pulls me in behind him. I'm not sure I'm prepared to be here and see all the players in their jock straps. "Ummm, I don't belong in here."

"You're with me. I belong in here."

We pass the empty workout room on the right. There's water running in the showers wherever that is and the main locker room at the end of the hall has music playing and lots of activity. He pulls me through an open door on the left and holds a finger up at me signaling to give him one minute. He leans out the doorway, "Martin! Carter's office." He grins and turns to me, "This is Carter our locker room manager and team assistant." He gestures to me, "This is Maggie. I think the two of you met briefly earlier."

"I had no idea who he was. It's nice to meet you," I reach out and shake his hand.

"Same," he laughs. "I'm sorry, that hoodie is horrible on you. I didn't do it, just fulfilling a player's request."

"I've been informed who did this," I nod.

There's scuffling in the hallway and Martin pops into the doorway. He turns behind him, "Come on guys, really?" He turns back and focuses, realizing I'm in the room, "Oh."

Drew gestures toward me, "This is Maggie. She wanted to meet you."

"Oh, okay. Hi Maggie, nice to meet you. Kris Martin," he extends his arm offering to shake hands.

"Why'd you tell the team I'm a stalker?" I ask using a fake stern tone, but he doesn't know that. Drew covers his mouth to hide his expression. "I'm not a stalker and friends should be able to share things in confidence."

Surprised, Martin replies, "I didn't tell the team you're a stalker."

From around the corner I hear, "You told me."

Then, "I definitely heard it from you."

"Yeah, he totally did. Seno and I were there, too."

Martin turns around, "Thanks for the support guys."

"Anytime," they all reply in unison.

"It's not like I told them all what he did, I keep secrets," Martin defends.

Interesting, "What did he do?"

"I'm not falling into that trap. I'd never do anything to get a teammate arrested or in trouble."

From the hallway, "Oh man, I wonder what Brandt did."

Martin turns to the hallway, "Enough from the peanut gallery."

"I wonder what Brandt did, too," I add.

Martin turns back to me, "You know, you were there."

"I'm sorry, I was where?"

"You were watching when he stripped naked."

"Oh, I think I know the night you're talking about."

"I'm sure you do. I don't think it's something you'd forget."

"It's not like you have a girlfriend or anything, so maybe you shouldn't be making fun," I continue.

Martin replies quick, "I have a woman."

"Since when? You never have a chick," loudly from the hallway.

"Shit," Martin scrubs his hand across his face.

I stand up, "And thank you for the hoodie."

"Geez, that's huge," Martin laughs.

"I think I'm going to climb into it with her," Drew says with a dirty grin.

I finally smile at Martin and laugh, "It's nice to finally meet you." I skip the handshake and give him a hug, leaning into his ear quietly, "Just messing with you."

Drew grabs my hand and pulls me in, "All good?"

"Yep," I give him a peck on the cheek.

He pulls me out the door to a lineup in the hallway, and introduces me to Houck, Cross, and Mason.

He leads the way out of the stadium, taking us up the ramp and exiting through the village gate.

I miss wearing my hoodie, but I get it now and it's not flattering. I'm a blob walking down the street with a hot ballplayer.

We get to his house and he takes me around to the side gate instead of up the front steps to the front door. He flips a switch and rows of lights strung over the yard come on. He clicks a few times on his phone and music starts to play through speakers in his yard...

"Siri."

"Yes, Master."

"Maggie's Playlist."

"Consider it done."

"Parallel Line," begins to play and he leads me to a large concrete pad in the middle of the yard with a brass inlay directing to true North. It's the same song that was playing last night. He wraps his arm around my waist and leads as he does so well, spiraling us around and holding me near. He always has eye contact with me while we're dancing, and I can't help but notice as the expressiveness of his eyes change. His deep blue eyes become deeper, bottomless, transparent, and a pathway to his heart. We dance and I'm thankful that my surveillance isn't hidden between us, even more that he doesn't care. The song changes to "Missing Piece," by Vance Joy. My unnecessary shenanigans don't bother him. I consider my actions and how they weren't necessary. He would've found me at the banquet, but me and my NVGs could've ruined it all. He gets me. He doesn't judge, though maybe he should sometimes. He did say I'm what he was searching for. I wonder what he's been missing? He pulls me in close and I rest my cheek against his chest. His fingers thread through my hair holding me there and his whole body relaxes, like he finally let go of everything he'd been hanging onto. The song changes again, "Caffeine," by Jack Kays starts to play and is interrupted by an alarm on his phone.

He grabs both of my hands and takes a step back, "Ready for dinner?"

"Yea, what are we having?" I ask.

"Lasagna," he leads me in through the back door of his house and the music keeps playing wherever we are. I slip the hoodie off since it's warm inside. The lights on the ground level all come on as we enter the room. The oven alarm on is going off as we walk into the kitchen and it smells amazing. There's a trivet, two pot holders, a kitchen towel, two plates, a serving utensil, and a note on the counter next to the oven. I notice the dining room table in the next room is set for two with candles, wine glasses, and three bottles of red wine, but missing the plates. Drew uses the pot holders to take the lasagna out of the oven, placing its bubbly cheesy dish of deliciousness on the trivet. I didn't think I was hungry, but now I am.

CHAPTER FORTY-SEVEN

Drew

I love my mom and everything she does for me, but sometimes she has her own motives. She left me a note with instructions for dinner:

Figlio Mio,
I set the oven timer to bake at the best time I could figure out and went with later rather than earlier to make sure you are home and it doesn't burn. Though, I do love the crispy bits around the edge of a lasagna and I'm not certain you can actually cook one to the point of it not being edible. Be careful not to burn yourself. I left everything you should need out at your fingertips and I've already set the table for you. There's also a green salad ready for you in the refrigerator and some of that balsamic vinaigrette I make that you love so much. There's no garlic bread because you want to be able to kiss later. I left the wine and the key on the

dining room table for you. I also left you a couple indi-
vidual tiramisus in the refrigerator, but I don't think
you'll get that far. Move them to the freezer and they'll
be good for a couple weeks. I hope your date is going
well. I can't wait to meet her.
Lo affetto
Mamma

Her lasagna is perfect as always. I let it cool while I collect the salad and vinaigrette from the refrigerator. "Would you like some salad with your lasagna?" I ask Maggie.

"Yes, please," she smiles. "Can I help with anything?"

"There's not much to do." I realize this is the first time I've had anyone over and my first dinner in the house that wasn't only reheated. It's a sense of home. Mom left the salad utensils in the salad bowl to keep them chilled. "You can plate the salad if you'd like," I set the bowl next to the plates and pull the plastic wrap off the top.

Maggie gives the salad a toss and places some neatly on both of the plates. She tastes the vinaigrette and makes yummy noises, "That stuff is perfect."

"It's my mom's. She made dinner for us. She likes to help out whenever she can and I don't turn down her food."

"I wouldn't either," she adds a healthy drizzle to her salad and mine.

I gaze over and laugh, "You should add more than that."

She smiles and gives both salads another drizzle, "I was trying to be on good behavior."

I shake my head, "The only good behavior involved with eating my mom's lasagna is cleaning the plate."

She watches me cut the lasagna, "I only want like half that much."

"You can eat however much you want and leave the rest," I reply, wondering if she eats it all or if I eat her leftovers. We each carry our plates to the table and examine what my mom has done. I light the candles she has ready in crystal domes and they send sparkling lights all around the room. I go to open the wine and find three bottles of my mom's favorite red that goes with her lasagna. Three bottles? A bit overkill for a weeknight. I open one and pour a glass for each of us, "This wine goes well with the lasagna. I hope you like it." Then I wonder if she's one of those who only drinks sparkling beverages, not everyone enjoys wine. I guess we will find out. I sit down and take a sip, and I'm comforted by my favorite things all with me in my home.

She swirls her glass and takes a sip, "I don't have much wine experience, but I'm wiling to give them a try."

"Get a bite of the lasagna with the flavor of the wine on your tongue."

I watch as she dives into the lasagna, the euphoria crossing her features, "This is better than lasagna."

I nod, refill my glass and top off hers as we eat together.

AFTER DINNER we clear the table. I move the tiramisu to the freezer and realize we went through two bottles of wine and opened the third. I'm relaxed and so is she, "Would you like to watch a movie with me?"

"Sure."

I lead her to the sofa and she sits down next to me, leaning against me. I put my arm around her shoulders, and she toes her shoes off, pulling her feet up underneath her.

"Do you like old movies?" I ask.

"Yea, the old black and whites have great drama and none of the special effects," she says.

I find an old black and white romance and turn the lights down. I love being close with her. We don't have to talk. We can be comfortable just being together in the same room.

"You're warm," she says and snuggles into me.

It's after 2am when I wake up suddenly and I'm not in my bed. I'm lying on my couch with Maggie sleeping in my arms. She's beautiful and peaceful. I spend a few minutes simply watching her sleep and wondering if she will wake up. I don't want to wake her, but I also want to go to bed. Spending the night on the couch is a bad idea, I always end up with a kink somewhere and that's not good for a professional athlete. I need to move to my bed and I don't want to leave her on the couch. She's really knocked out. I hold her tight and get up with her in my arms. She doesn't wake up but she's breathing. I carry her up the stairs to my room and set her down on my bed. This was a bad idea. Simply seeing her in my bed—I'm instantly hard. I take my shirt off, toe off my shoes, and dig through my dresser drawer for a pair of pajama pants. I find a pair of lightweight jersey pajama pants and change into those from my jeans. Usually, I sleep naked. I climb into my bed and pull the blanket up over the both of us. She mumbles something, but nothing I can determine. She mumbles again and says something about Frank, but she never wakes up. Who's Frank? I'll have to add that to the list of puzzles associated with this amazing woman. I roll over to her and put my arm over her, holding her to me. Hoping she doesn't freak out when she wakes up in my bed.

CHAPTER FORTY-EIGHT

Maggie

My feet are cold, but it's not time to get up yet and I don't want to open my eyes. I move my feet around trying to get them tucked back into my warm snuggly blanket. The blanket's not snuggly. The blanket is soft, but thin and has holes in it. I rub the blanket between my fingers. It might be an Afghan. This isn't my blanket. I pull my feet up closer to my body for warmth, and I find a warm body that's not mine. I should really open my eyes. I inventory my clothing and I'm still dressed, but there's a strong arm around my waist and warm breath on my neck. I open my eyes, but it's pitch black. I sit up, trying to focus on my surroundings.

"I brought you to bed with me when I woke and we were both asleep on the couch. It's okay, Maggie," a tender and deep male voice comforts me. I've never been in this position before. I remember sitting with Drew on his sofa and watching a movie, but not much of the movie. Am I in Drew's bed?

I reach out to the man I'm in bed with and find bare skin. "You're warm. My feet are cold."

He tosses the blanket that's covering us away and folds down the blankets, "Let's get you warmed up." I lean in closer trying to find him by touch and kiss his lips. I crawl into his bed and pull the thick warm blankets up around my neck. He gets under the blankets with me, "Come to me, Maggie. Please." I roll over to him and he puts his arm under my neck, cradling me against him. His bare chest is my pillow and I can't help but explore it. I graze my fingers across his chest, finding each defined muscle and discovering the textures of his skin. He groans and I put my leg over his, burying my foot between his legs. "Maggie, are you awake?"

"Uh huh."

"Tell me who I am."

"You're Drew Brandt. The only man for me since junior high..."

"Maggie?"

CHAPTER FORTY-NINE

Drew

No response beyond a sigh. I kiss her forehead and hold her tight, hoping to get a few more hours of sleep with Maggie in my arms.

I WAKE up alone but the bed is still warm. I didn't consider if it would be too much for her to wake up in my bed, in a room where she'd never been before. The fact that I have the light blacked out probably just adds to her confusion. I open the blackouts a few inches to let some light in. Did she leave? "Maggie?" I call out. I should get up anyway, but I don't want to if I can have Maggie just a little bit longer. There are footsteps on the stairs and my beautiful woman appears in the doorway.

"I had to find the bathroom," she says as she crawls back in bed with me and pulls the blankets up around her neck.

"There's a bathroom right here, you didn't have to go downstairs."

"I couldn't see, so I followed the light from downstairs," she replies as she reaches for me and finds my hard cock. She stops silent.

"Sorry, just ignore that," I say hoping she doesn't run from me. Sex is not my intent, though it is on my mind.

She doesn't pull away, she wraps her hand around it and seems to be measuring it with her hand. My cock gets harder in response. "Oh," she starts over with whatever she was doing. She rolls away from me and shimmies around. Then crawls back to me and lays on top of me. My hands immediately at her hips find her pants are gone, and her panties are small and lacy. "Hi," she says and gazes at me with bright eyes.

"Hi," I say wondering if it's an invitation or if she's just getting comfortable. "I think we should take this part off too," I say and grab the bottom hem of her top, pulling it off over her head. The lace of her bra rubs against me and I want a view of her. I need to see the body I've held and get a glimpse of her lacy attire. I run my finger under the top of her panties, "Will you show me these sexy little things?" She giggles and climbs out of bed. I open the blackouts all the way for more light. She grabs the Afghan from the floor and wraps it around her. She's standing there simply staring at me, her feet dancing around. She has my complete attention and has since the moment I saw her at the banquet.

She laughs, "What do you want to see?" She turns in a circle. She flashes me her right side, then her left, then turns around and drops the blanket to her hips revealing her black lace bra and her seductive shape before letting it fall to the floor and exposing her black lace thong. She's inherently slender, but not skinny, and absolutely gorgeous. Sexy as hell in the skimpy black lace. I wouldn't have been able to keep my hands off of her if I'd known she was wearing it.

I crook my finger at her and she shakes her head. I crook my finger again and nod, and she climbs back on top of me with my cock hard between her thighs. I run my hands up and down her sides. I want to eat her up, but I don't want to push her. I roll her underneath me and take control. I kiss her jawline and make a trail around to her ear and down her neck, her body rewarding me with her reactions. I stop and rest my chin on my hands between her breasts.

"Why'd you stop?" She asks.

"I don't want to go too fast."

CHAPTER FIFTY

Maggie

"Too fast?" Comes out almost as a squeal. "Are you kidding me? I've compared every guy to you since junior high school and I'm still single. What does that tell you?"

"Um, well..."

I cut him off, "Nobody compares to my image of you except you."

He gets a huge grin, "I was going to say that me now is better than junior high school me."

"I can't know that for sure. I don't have the research data. Most likely parts of you are better now and other parts were better then. Even in my dreams I never get to the good stuff, not even a kiss until it was the real thing." Damn it! I need to learn to keep my mouth shut. Statistics are fine, but the rest? Ah! I'm out of here. I start to get up, but...

"Oh no, you're not going anywhere," he says and changes his position so that he's lying across me and I can't get up.

"Let me go!" I squeal and attempt to kick my legs.

"Not until you listen to me for a minute," he stays still and patient.

I growl, "Fine. What?"

"I want you to know me now. The man I am. What my dreams and desires are. What I believe my future will be like. My true heart. The intentions in my hands when I touch you. And, where it all comes from. I'm not that kid anymore and you aren't a kid anymore either." He stops and gazes at me as I do my best to appear uninterested.

"I listened. Are you done? Can I go now?" I'd cross my arms across my chest if I could.

"No. There's more."

"Then get on with it. I don't have all day,"

"Okay, bossy britches. I want to know you—everything about you inside and out. What made you the way you are? All of your personal and business goals and timelines and statistics. Is there anything that you trust your heart with over the odds? Why me and if not me, how do I change that? I want to know why you make me want to give you everything and take care of you by just being you. I don't want to be a baseball player conquest. Oh, and who the fuck is Frank? He has to go because you're mine now."

I laugh at him out load and I probably shouldn't because that's probably supposed to be his angry face.

"You're laughing at me?"

I nod and continue to laugh. "Frank isn't going anywhere."

"You're here with me. What would he think about that?" He says, as serious as a heart attack.

"He's probably not liking it much right now but he'll get over it." He glares at me and I continue, "Come on, let's get up and go get coffee. I need caffeine. Oh, and so I know, do you have rules about eating, drinking, sex, anything on game days?" I slide out from under him and pull my leggings on.

He follows my lead and gets up, pulling a T-shirt on and glaring at me, "Coach has suggested guidelines, but I do what I want. Am I allowed to change my pants with you in the room?"

"Oh yeah, that's fine," I nod and stand there watching. "Nothing I haven't seen before from a distance."

"You're going to drive me crazy," he says as he strips his lower half and turns away from me to put on his boxer briefs. Damn he has a nice ass.

"That just means you love me," I say and try to suck it back in.

"What?"

"I said, that just means you need more of me."

"HHhhmmmm," he puts his sneakers on and I try to find my top.

"Where did you throw my shirt to?"

He shrugs and scans the room, he bends over and picks it up and tosses it at me, "I can get you a clean shirt, if you want."

"Do you keep a collection of women's clothes just in case?" I can't help myself.

"No. You could wear one of my T-shirts. I've never had a woman over here and, honestly, I can't remember the last time I had a woman in any bed," he says frustrated.

"Okay."

"Okay, what?" He flails his arm in frustration.

"I'll take a clean T-shirt."

He opens a drawer, grabs a shirt and throws it at me in a way that only a baseball player would, "Thank you." I check the size and what the graphic on it is. I might spontaneously combust, it's a shirt from his minor league stint with the

Lancaster Landsharks. I try to maintain my excitement, and slip it on over my head. It fits me perfect and there's no way it fits him. It's soft and stretchy like a worn old concert shirt. As reserved as possible, I ask, "Can I keep it? I'm guessing it won't fit you." I model it for him.

"Yeah, it looks good on you."

"Thank you." I run downstairs and slip into my shoes. I dig my brush out of my backpack and run it through my hair.

He grabs a baseball cap off the wall, "Are you going to wear your hoodie?"

"That huge thing?"

"Yea. You always wear a hoodie to go get your coffee."

I shrug, "Things change."

"Leave it here, I have plans for it," he says.

"Okay," I say and follow his lead to the front door. Caroline is going to have a fit when we walk up for coffee.

He stops when we get to the sidewalk and grabs my hand, entwining his fingers with mine and kissing my knuckles.

"Do you have time to walk me home after we get coffee?"

"Definitely."

We walk to the coffee stand and when it comes into view there's a line at least ten people deep with only Caroline there. "Hold on one second," I stop walking and grab my phone.

Me: On our way to get coffee.

Me: You look busy.

Caroline: Yep.

Caroline: Play the online order game and just drop the money in the tip jar.

Caroline: Wait... OUR?

Caroline: Where are you?

Me: 10 o'clock for you.

Caroline: Okay. I know the orders.
Caroline: Give me five minutes.
Caroline: We have some catching up to do.
Me: Oh yeah.
Me: Thank you.

I turn to Drew, "We need to hang back a few minutes while she makes our coffees. Payment goes in the tip jar."

"Is that code?" He asks.

"It's how we pretend it was an online order and skip the line when it's like this."

"Clever. It's the chick in 80's workout gear, right?"

"Yeah, that's my roommate, Caroline."

"I'd gathered that info already coming here to get coffee. I just hadn't confirmed you were the hoodie girl until yesterday. I was pretty sure though."

"How sure?" I inquire.

"Are you looking for numbers?" He chuckles.

"Yes," I say decisively and wonder what he bases it on.

"85% give or take, my gut isn't exactly scientific deduction," he chuckles.

"Fair. And the hoodie is what connected the 'adorable hoodie girl' to the NVGs?" I question. He handled the caveat well.

"Yeah, especially when you shined the light from your phone toward you," he chuckled.

"I can be such a klutz sometimes," I shake my head. "I was trying to stay in the dark and I didn't have my NVGs with me that night. Caroline wanted me to stop, she was afraid you'd put a restraining order on me and we'd have to move because we live too close."

Caroline: Ready.

"Our coffees are ready," we walk up to the stand and grab them from the online orders.

"Thank you," I drop a few bucks in the tip jar and Drew drops a $20 in after me.

I turn to him, "$20?"

"Two coffees and special service. Plus, she makes the best coffee I've ever had."

"That's what I keep telling her! And that guy who covers for her, just skip it and walk away," I laugh.

"Yeah, I learned that the hard way. How can they be so different when it's the same coffee?"

"That's what scares me the most," I nod.

Me: I'm taking him to our place.

Caroline: Don't do it.

Me: It'll be fine.

Caroline: What's your motive?

Me: I need to introduce him to Frank.

Caroline: I don't think that's necessary.

Me: It's very necessary.

Caroline: Good luck.

Caroline: I was working on biscuit recipes last night.

Caroline: Don't mess with what I've got going on in the kitchen.

Me: Yes, ma'am.

Caroline: There are 4 different batches. You can have none, or one of each and share. I need feedback.

Me: And suddenly I'm a guinea pig.

Caroline: You and your professional athlete to be clear.

Me: Thanks for that.

Caroline: They should be the perfect complement to your coffee.

I gaze up at him, "Let's go to my place." I grab his hand and lead the way.

Drew stares at his coffee, "What does she do to this coffee that makes me so happy?"

"I've asked and all she'll say is that she makes it with love. Just wait, she has deemed us taste testers. I missed out on fresh baked biscuits because I was with you last night."

"Is that a complaint?"

"No, and the fact that it's not a complaint—you should take that as a monumental compliment," I nod. "Her cookies are delicious."

We get to my building and walk to my unit at the end on the left. I unlock the door and bring in packages that have been delivered for Caroline, there's always packages for Caroline. I turn to Drew still standing outside, "Come on in." I reach for him and stretch up on my tiptoes to give him a quick kiss on the lips.

He wraps his arms around my waist and holds me close, "Do you want to come over to my place tonight after the game?"

"What do you have in mind?"

"We can have leftovers, we can order takeout, we can pick up where we left off this morning, we can skip straight to dessert, we could have a sleep over—you name it."

I pull him in, so I can close the door and stop worrying about Frank scampering out. I survey the scene and realize how different my two-bedroom, one bath girl space apartment is compared to his perfectly put together and professionally decorated two story house. You'd never find a movie poster push pinned to the wall at his place, let alone a kitchen left with the mess from baking dozens of biscuits, and a hamster that lives in the bedroom. Two of which I'm highlighting on this stop—yay.

"We have a couple of important things to do while we're here before we move on to plan for later tonight. Are you ready?"

He shakes his head, "I think so."

"Have your coffee ready," I take him into my kitchen of mix and match hand-me-downs. "There are 4 different batches of cookies and we can share one cookie from each batch. Caroline wants feedback."

"Half of four cookies each?"

"Yes, good math."

"I need more information."

"Of course. Caroline is perfecting her biscuit recipe because she intends to sell them at the coffee stand when she takes it over or opens her own. It's the beginning of the business plan she has, but the goal is to share the best coffee with everyone and add the biscuits."

"So we're tasting cookies and giving her feedback to help the greater mankind have better coffee?"

"Yes."

"Sounds like a good cause, I'm in."

I break one biscuit from each of the four batches in half, "We have to leave her feedback on each cookie and tell her which one we like best."

"Okay," he nods and we start trying cookies. I make notes as I go on each regarding the texture, how buttery they are, sweetness, whatever strikes me on that cookie. Drew is done with all four and I'm just making my notes on the first one.

"Do you need paper to leave feedback or would you like to give me some notes for her?"

"Number three was the best one, followed by four, two, and one in that order."

"Why?"

"They were all perfectly fine, number three just stood out."

I shake my head and try the rest of the cookies to end up picking them in the same order. However, I think it's the balance of texture, crumbliness, and butter that makes it. Of course, that pretty much sums up the cookie.

"Do we get more cookies?" He asks.

"No, that's all we were allowed."

"That's just teasing me," he drinks the rest of his coffee. "And they go so good with the coffee."

"So you're in agreement with her business plan and adding the biscuits to the coffee stand?"

"100%."

"It's so sexy when you use your numbers," I stretch up and give him a kiss. "Now for the second important thing we need to do here today. I'm taking you into my bedroom and we're going to lay on my bed, but it's not for any reason you're thinking."

"How can you be sure?"

"Statistics. You have to have all of the factors involved for it to be a possibility and you don't."

"Okay," he braces himself.

I take him into my disaster of a bedroom. "Wait until I tell you it's okay to lay down." I sit on the edge of my bed and make sure I have Frank's whereabouts, "Okay, snuggle in here with me please." I pat the bed.

Drew glares at me and goes along with it, "Now what?"

"Hold on," I grab Frank from where he was nesting in the end of my pillowcase. "This is Frank," I set him on the blanket covering my chest and his little nose twitches, taking in the new smells. He crawls up to my neck and snuggles in between us.

"Frank is your hamster?"

"Yes, he's a teddy bear hamster."

"He's just loose in your bedroom?" He asks with a note of concern.

"Yeah, it seems to work best. He breaks out of cages. He's mostly on the bed up near my pillow somewhere. He's really good about doing his business in the same place all the time. We have an agreement, I leave him a paper towel to do his business on and he chews it up around the edges making a mess. It's still in the working stages since I thought he was gone for over a month but then I found him when I was trying to figure out the NVGs."

"Got it. What's next on the list?"

"That's it for now," I move Frank and roll over snuggling into Drew.

"I like this."

"I thought you might," I say as my hands wander up his shirt. "I'm still wearing the panties from earlier."

He checks his phone, "I don't have enough time left before I need to be at the stadium. But we can pick up where we left off tonight if you'd like."

"I'd like," I grin.

He gazes into my eyes, "I'd rather spend the rest of the day and night with you, but I have to get to work."

"I understand. There's adulting to be done," he squeezes me and climbs out of bed. "I'll see you at the stadium." I get up and follow him to the door stretching up for my goodbye kiss.

"See you tonight, Maggie," His voice low and heady. He turns and leaves.

And I freak out because I don't have anything to wear tonight. That was the only sexy bra and panties I own! When did I become this person who's not happy to just pull on her oversized hoodie and go?

Me: Help. Again.

Me: First, Drew and I agree that biscuit 3 is the winner.

Me: Second, I need sexy underwear for my date tonight.

Caroline: I picked biscuit 3 too, so it must be the one.

Me: However all 4 were delicious.

Caroline: Thank you.

Caroline: Did you do the deed?

Me: No. But he saw my bra and panties.

Caroline: Ummm... How?

Me: One thing at a time.

Me: It was a great night.

Me: We fell asleep together on his couch and I woke up in his bed. Clothed.

Me: Lasagna, red wine, candles, dancing, cuddling

Caroline: But no sex.

Me: No, but I did touch it through his PJ pants this morning.

Caroline: And?

Me: He's fucking huge. I thought he was big. I touched him and he got harder.

Me: Anyway, we're having a sleepover tonight at his place.

Caroline: A planned sleepover?

Me: Yes.

Caroline: You need more than sexy undies. You need a sexy nightie or something.

Me: I have my leggings and a T-shirt.

Caroline: No. Just. No.

Caroline: Were there any packages delivered for me?

Me: Yes, a few small bags.

Caroline: Open them up and see what we got. I'm expecting more than that.

Me: I don't need to open your packages.

Caroline: Just do it.

I gather the packages on the coffee table and open each of them carefully. They're all lightweight. Panties. Sexy panties. Sexy bras. Lingerie. I check the sizes and they're all my size.

Me: How did you know I'd need this stuff?

Caroline: You're dating Drew Brandt.

Caroline: Men like lingerie.

Caroline: It's good for you to be sexy.

Caroline: It's a little something extra to make him want you more.

Caroline: Go try them on and bag up the ones you don't want. You have time to wash them before your date tonight. Oh and there are more still to be delivered.

Caroline: I hope the black lace and velour nightie is as sexy on as it looked online.

Me: I don't think that one is here yet.

Me: The teal satin slip nightie is gorgeous.

Caroline: I thought that would go well with your skin tone.

Caroline: Don't forget to pack for your sleepover. Sexy stuff and clothes for tomorrow too. Toothbrush.

Me: How many thongs does one girl need?

Caroline: At least 5 when they're 5 for $10.

Me: Thank you to you and your crystal ball.

Caroline: You'll hook me up with a ball player someday it's only a matter of time.

Me: Oh yeah, I met Cross, Mason, Houck, and Martin last night.

Caroline: It's already starting.

Caroline: Remember me when you get invited to a player's party.

Me: I'm just going to get them hooked on your coffee
and biscuits.
Caroline: Best way to a man's heart is through his
stomach.
Caroline: Now, go try on your sexy undies.

I go through the lingerie piece by piece, trying each on and modeling in front of my mirror. The stark difference from this to my hoodie is devastating. The hoodie is warm and cozy and comforting. But the sexy satin and lace gives me confidence and makes me happy. What was I thinking? Though I'm not sure about this crotchless pair of panties or the pair that have an open heart at my ass, the latter seems like inviting something I'm not interested in. Though they are cute. I toss what I want to keep into the wash real quick.

I get to work updating my numbers for my thesis and set up my projections to run.

I dump my backpack out and pack a small bag with my toothbrush, a pair of socks, and clothes for tomorrow. Not taking any chance of having cold feet again. Once my laundry is dry I add my lingerie and shove the small bag into the bottom of my backpack. I drop my lightweight hoodie, brush, and a book, in on top of it. My new Brandt jersey is ready to go for the game today and I need another one of Caroline's magical coffees to relax and be human again.

Drew: I miss you already.
Drew: I can't wait for tonight.
Me: Me too.
Drew: Can you be here before batting practice?
Me: I'll try my best.
Drew: 😶

I'm going to need more energy.

Me: What would I need to do to get another of your magical elixirs delivered to me in the next 5-10 minutes?
Caroline: You don't ask for much, do you?
Caroline: It takes me 2 minutes to make it.
Me: I understand if you can't.
Me: I'm going to need something to pick me up and get me through tonight.
Caroline: Brown Chicken Brown Cow
Me: If you could see me, you'd know my eyes are rolling hard right now.
Caroline: Sending your coffee with my lackey.
Me: Have him leave it on the step please.
Caroline: Done.
Caroline: Have fun tonight!
Me: Thank you! I'm planning on it.

I take a quick shower, and get dressed. I put on a teal satin thong, its matching teal satin bra, a fitted navy-blue camisole, and my snug fitting jeans. I slide into my sneakers and throw my jersey on when I'm ready to walk out the door. I open the door, grab my coffee, and put my backpack on. Ready to roll in plenty of time to make batting practice.

Me: I'm walking up to the gate now.
Me: Dropping my backpack off at my desk.
Drew: 👍

The elevator up to the press box takes forever. I get to the press box and find Drew sitting in my chair with his knees pulled up to his chest and spinning.
"It's fun isn't it?"

"Yes," he laughs and slows his spin until he stops. He starts to stand and flops back down in the chair dizzy from spinning.

I laugh, "You were going fast."

"Yeah, and I was spinning for a few minutes while waiting for you. I guess you're going to have to come to me," He smiles.

I walk over to him, dropping my backpack under my desk, and sit on his lap facing him. I wrap my arms around his neck, "How's this?"

"This is very nice," he says and takes a deep breath.

I move slightly and he groans, pulling my face to his and claiming my lips. Tugging until I open for him, he slips his tongue in my mouth and pulls me into him by my very soul. He gets hard beneath me and I want to rub against his cock. Breathless with need I take my lips from his and gaze into his eyes as I lick my lips. He reaches for me, hugging me and whispers in my ear, "I want you."

I squeeze him and whisper back, "I'm already yours."

He leans back and gazes at me, gesturing for me to get up, "I have to get to BP. But I'll be thinking about you."

I nod, "I'll be down at field level to watch BP."

"Tonight it's us," he yells back at me as he leaves the press box.

I get set up for the game and grab a bottle of water on my way down to the field level.

I get settled by the dugout to watch BP and Drew waves at me then disappears into the dugout, reappearing a couple minutes later and coming up to me in the stands. He places one of his baseball caps on my head, "I don't want you getting sunburn on your beautiful face." He gives me a quick peck and takes off for the field.

A few minutes into batting practice a woman walks over

and sits next to me, "Hi, I'm Sherry Seno. I heard you're dating Brandt and you work here in the stadium?"

"Maggie," I extend my hand to shake hers. "Yes, that's right," I don't know this woman.

"I used to come to batting practice every day and never miss a game, but with the baby I've learned I can't always be on my schedule. It's getting better though and I can bring her to a lot of the games with me."

"Oh, exciting to have a little girl to get into baseball! A buddy to go to the games with, too."

"Hopefully. So how long have you known Drew?"

"We went to school together from junior high on. I was scorekeeper for his teams," I offer.

"I never did the scorekeeping thing. I'm too busy yelling at the opposing team and cheering on my guy."

"It's a different perspective. I can't yell during the games while I'm doing stats and keeping my scorebooks, but I watch every play."

"No, I couldn't do that. I've never in my life been quiet at a game," she laughs. "Seno likes to know I'm here and listens for me. Some things are just unexpected, you know?"

"Most things can be predicted, but I get what you're saying there's not data quantifying the values of love. I think that's what makes it so scary. The risk of the unknown."

"What position are you in at the stadium?"

"I'm the team statistician, but it's just a part-time thing. It works well for me while I'm working on my thesis," I reply.

"That must make it challenging to make ends meet," she shakes her head.

"It's not bad with a roommate. Caroline has been my roommate since freshman year, she's great and watches out for me. She graduated with her degree in business and is working on having her own business. We do well together."

"She could probably use some investors. What kind of business?"

"A coffee stand that also has fresh baked biscuit-like cookies. She makes the best coffee I've had and her biscuits melt in your mouth."

"She'd be perfect for Chase Cross."

"I'm sorry?"

"You didn't hear any of this," she glares at me for confirmation and I nod. "His girl left him for a job and isn't coming back. He hasn't told anyone. Everyone thinks she's on assignment."

"Oh, no. That's horrible. He seems like such a sweetheart."

"He is. He's my buddy. He's perfect for Caroline. He loves cookies. He needs someone that wants him and will love him who's not a player chaser."

"She does have big plans for the coffee stand. She wants to sell franchises and get her coffee and biscuits worldwide. I know it sounds underwhelming, but if you tried her coffee you'd get it."

"It's that good?"

I nod. "She's working at the stand over in the village. She's the one that always looks like she's working out in the 1980's."

"What?"

"It's her thing. She stands out."

"Oh yeah... they totally match," she nods. "I'll take care of it."

CHAPTER FIFTY-ONE

Drew

I text my mom on my walk to the stadium:

Me: Thank you for making dinner and getting things ready for me.

Me: Your lasagna was perfect as always and she loved it.

Mom: You're welcome, dear.

Mom: You know I'm always happy to help whenever I can.

Me: Yes, and I appreciate it.

Me: We probably didn't need three bottles of wine.

Mom: Did the third bottle get opened?

Me: Yes.

Mom: Then you needed it.

Me: Still, seems like a bit much.

Me: Especially with no bread.

Mom: Just trying to help.

Me: Help get us drunk?

Mom: Whatever gets me grandchildren.

Me: We just started dating.

Mom: You've known each other for years.

Mom: It's fine.

Mom: You should enjoy yourselves.

Mom: Get naked.

Mom: Share some pleasure.

Me: I'm going now.

Mom: Okay. If you need help or tips let me know.

Me: Love you, mom.

The older my mom gets, the more words I get from her that I don't want to hear. She doesn't need to know the truth.

"WHAT ARE Maggie and Sherry talking about?" I ask Seno as we stand behind the backstop.

"Sherry likes to get to know the player's women. No telling what they're talking about. Girl talk," Seno shrugs. "Don't worry about it. So, how's it going with you two? I heard she's got a smart mouth on her."

"She definitely does. Drives me crazy."

"Congrats on finding the one."

"I didn't say that."

"That's what I heard," Seno walks off for his turn to hit.

IT's game time and all I can think about is Maggie. It's comfortable, fun, and unexpected when we're together. I have no clue what words are going to come out of her mouth next or when she might introduce me to a hamster. She's a quirky unpredictable conundrum of analytics, femininity, and self-preservation. I'm interested in discussing baseball and her thesis with her, however I'm also concerned that we may have differing opinions so I'm making that wait as long as possible though I'm aware she'll have statistics to back up every word she says. I was surprised to find her in skimpy lace panties, don't get me wrong—I appreciate them very much and I'm looking forward to ripping them off of her. I wonder what she's got hiding under her jeans and jersey today? I love that I can look up at her and there she is wearing my jersey. She's wearing a top that's a little bit revealing today with ruching between her breasts—it's different than her normal crew neck shirts. I hope she sits on my lap like that again later tonight, I wanted to have sex with her right there in the press box. Not a good idea, but when my cock can detect her heat through her jeans? Decisions aren't always made with the right head, and my cock was trying to be the bigger of the two at that moment. I need to focus on the game and stop rubbing my hard dick against the dugout rail.

I'm hitting third in the lineup today, right after Martin. Things go to shit pretty quick in the top of the first when Kranston, our starting pitcher, drops to the ground to avoid being hit by a fastball off the bat of the opposing team's leadoff hitter, and is removed from the game with a twisted ankle. The bull pen takes over for the rest of the game. Bottom of the first inning and I'm at bat with Prince on second base, Martin struck out. Prince gets picked off attempting to steal third and I work the count, hitting a grounder but end up out at first.

It's been a busy game backing up the bull pen on defense. My uniform is covered in dirt from diving for the ball. Martin and I have turned two double plays and we're only halfway through the game. I strike out on my second at bat.

Seno grabs me as he's walking out onto the field to catch for the fifth inning, "Keep your focus. She will be there when the game is over. And trust me, women like winners." He stares into my eyes and nods waiting for my response.

I nod back, "Understood." He pats me on the back and moves on into his position.

On my third at bat I smash a homer into the left field grandstands knocking in Prince and Martin, making the score 3-2 Seals and taking over the lead in the eighth inning. I run the bases and as I turn the corner at third I gaze up towards the press box to find Maggie on her feet and clapping. She smiles and turns around to show me and everybody else her jersey. I point at her and run across home plate. Forty thousand fans in the stands and all I see is her. Houck closes it out in the top of the ninth inning, Seals win.

The on-field reporter grabs me and I take the time to do their interview, "Brandt, great job tonight. You drove in every run of the game for this win and turned three perfectly executed double plays with your first baseman. Is this just a lucky game for you or do you attribute this to something specific?"

I grin and nod at the word lucky, "Martin and I have been spending a lot of time working on the mechanics of double plays with a goal of speed and accuracy, so the only luck there is that we get the ball."

"What about your hitting? It's been noted your hitting has improved this season and specifically the last few batting practices has been more aggressive."

"I always do my best for the team. In addition to being challenged by my teammates, Captain Seno is always in our ears with support when we need it."

"And lastly, the booth noticed you pointing to the press box when you crossed home plate tonight and relayed to me that they've never seen you do that. What can you tell me about that?"

Should I simply wag it off or how do I answer this without going into it too much? I stare at the ground for a second and take a deep breath, "You'll be seeing that from now on."

"Thank you, Brandt. There you have it, practice makes perfect and a little bit of mystery from our second baseman Drew Brandt."

Running into the locker room Seno nods at me, "Good job." I nod in return and give him a high five. Representing the team in the community I'm fine with, but spontaneous live interviews are not my thing.

I STAND in the doorway to the press box and Maggie's sitting at her laptop working away, with multiple notebooks open and occasionally stopping to make a note with a colored pencil. "Hi," I call out to her not wanting to scare her, and get no response. I walk closer and realize she has her Air Pods in when I see her tapping her feet and mouthing words while she's working.

Me: Are you ready?
Maggie: Yep. Waiting for you in the press box.
Me: I'm standing 10 feet away from you.

She turns and pulls her pods out quickly when she sees me. She smiles bright, "Trying to stay caught up on everything, but I already submitted everything for tonight's game."

She closes her laptop and notebooks, and packs all her pencils in a pouch, then packs it all away in her backpack.

I grab her around the waist and pull her to me, "I've been thinking about you all day." I kiss her lips sweetly, "Can we go home now?"

She nods and I take her backpack with my other hand. "You smashed that ball in the eighth," she says.

"It did feel good."

"And the three double plays were effortless. I already knew you and Martin would get three DPs tonight."

"How'd you know?"

"UUuumm, I've been projecting numbers for different stats and players for my thesis and one of the things I'm tracking is Brandt/Martin double plays. You average at least two per game and you were due for a game with three, the stat was down to an average of 2.1 DPs per game and it's been sitting at 2.25 DPs or more per game for the last month."

"But it's not shared anywhere else?"

"Not that stat, no. But part of my job is to share patterns when I find them. I never know if they're taken into consideration or not, but I emailed the coach about other stats I'm projecting for my thesis and the next day you were following Martin in the lineup. I think that was all me."

"So, the Cross/Seno change was probably you too."

"I did send a note on that as well."

"Why are you tracking and projecting me and Martin, and Cross/Seno?"

"Part of the chemistry argument for my thesis. Players who are training and playing together are potentially adding the chemistry of their relationship to their skillset as baseball players as well as a higher level of trust."

I stop and consider her words, "Interesting, because I

should treat all my teammates the same on the field, but there are definitely balls I'd throw to Martin that I'd never consider throwing to any of my other teammates."

"Trust in the teammate and his skills, based on the chemistry of your relationship... My bet is you play catch intuitively and that translates to the game."

"And of course you have numbers to back that up."

"Somewhat. It's hard to generate numbers on chemistry and relationships. Though as soon as I figure that out Caroline and I are starting a matchmaking service."

I laugh out loud and then stop, "You're serious."

"Yep. But thesis first."

Absolutely unpredictable. I entangle my fingers with hers and she squeezes, holding on tight. "What would you like to do tonight? Are you hungry?"

"I'm not hungry, but I've been thinking about that tiramisu from last night. Maybe some dessert later?"

"That sounds perfect." I lean in and whisper in her ear, "Maybe you can be my pre-dessert treat?"

She giggles and nods. "Okay," she says in an unsure tone.

Not wanting to push her, "You can tell me no."

"I'll never tell you no," she smiles and picks up speed.

We get home and I lead her up the front steps of my house. Opening the door and pulling her in behind me, I slam the door closed and press her back to the door with my body. All I've wanted, needed, all day is her. I raise her hands above her head and hold her wrists in my hand as I nibble at her neck and ear. Unable to control myself I rub my hard cock against her hip. She releases a breath and wraps her legs around me, pushing her heat against my cock.

"Drew," she says out of breath and attempting to tug her hands free. "Please."

I press my lips to hers, tasting her desire as it mixes with mine. She pulls one hand free and immediately reaches for my belt. Squeezing her hand between us to unbuckle my belt and unbutton my jeans. When the zipper goes down there's no containing my hard cock. Fuck me, her delicate hand shoving its way in and grasping my cock, stroking it, I get harder. I release her other hand and she holds on, moving both hands to my shoulders and kissing her way from my shoulder up my neck. I need her in my bed. I carry her up the stairs to my room and climb onto my bed with her clinging to me.

I stop and take a deep breath, gazing into her eyes, "Hi." Is all I can put together.

She smiles and her eyes light up, "Hi." She bites her lower lip.

I try to pull some sanity together, "I'll never hurt you. You can always tell me no."

All she says is, "Please." She grabs the bottom hem of my shirt and pulls it off over my head. She kicks her shoes off and they go flying across the room.

I smile, filled with pleasure, as she pushes my jeans down and I toe off my shoes to assist. She unbuttons her jeans and slithers out of them while lying underneath me. She pulls her arms out of her jersey and she's so sexy lying there in her skimpy satin thong and camisole. I want to please her but I have to have her wrapped around me. I push my briefs off and rub my hard naked cock against her pussy. She's already wet for me. I reach for my nightstand and grab the box of condoms out, taking one and leaving the box accessible. I hand her the condom and she takes my cock in her hand, examining it closely. She kisses my tip and licks her lips. Fuck me. She licks around the head of my cock and takes it into her mouth, lightly sucking on me, "Fuck." She giggles at the reaction she draws from me and takes me deeper in her mouth, stroking me with her soft wet lips and teasing me with her tongue as she swirls it around my tip. I palm the back of her head and move with her, fucking her mouth. She has one hand around my shaft and the other reached down between her legs touching herself—"In my bed, I'm the only one that gets you off. There's no touching yourself here." She continues to pleasure herself with two fingers sliding up and down between her folds. "Maggie." She ignores me and sucks harder on my cock taking me into her throat. I grab her hand away from her wet pleasure and she stops with my cock deep in her mouth and stares up at me. She pulls off of my cock, sucking hard. I grab her feet, dragging her down flat and farther on the bed. I glide my hands from her hips to her breasts, squeezing gently while I place a line of gentle kisses from her naval to her chin. Stopping to appreciate her soft sweet lips I kiss the right edge of her lips and then the left, give her lower lip a tug with my teeth, lick her upper lip, then claim her lips as mine while I shove my cock into her sex rough and hard. Fuck she's tight and wet and meeting my every move with her own desirous needs. "Damn it, Maggie. You're perfect for me. I can't control myself, I just want more," I say and I pound my huge cock into her tight hole. "We need to stop. I need to take care of you first."

"Drew! Oh Drew!"

I start to pull out.

"No! Please just fuck me more," she begs.

I stroke into her a few more selfish times and as I'm pulling out she shatters around me and I cum instantly at the intensity. I stay still and spent as I gaze at her satisfied expression. My beautiful Maggie. I lie down next to her and pull her into me wanting to hold her forever. Her body still trembling in pleasure.

I WAKE up two hours later alone in my bed. I hope she didn't leave. I didn't intend to hurt her or use her. I want her to stay. Her shoes are still on the floor and her clothes are thrown everywhere. She can't be far naked. I set Maggie's playlist to play throughout the house and go in search of her, finding her in the kitchen wearing the huge hoodie and defrosting tiramisu.

I walk up behind her and wrap my arms around her, "Everything okay?"

"Everything is perfect," she beams at me and takes the tiramisu out of the microwave. She digs her spoon in and offers me the first bite. I take the spoon from her and feed the whole dessert to her one bite at a time, kissing her between each bite.

She's wearing the huge hoodie. I can't get over it. I truly could fit in there with her.

I bite my lip, "Round two!"

She laughs scraping the remains of the tiramisu from the dish with her finger.

I suck her finger into my mouth and toss the container and spoon into the sink. I throw her over my shoulder and she squeals, "Drew!" She kicks and laughs as I carry her back up the stairs to my bedroom.

I throw her down on my bed, "I don't know what it is with you and the hoodies, but I'm climbing in there with you to find out."

"What?" She screeches. "How?" She laughs and fidgets around.

I put the hoodie on with her in it and facing me. It's soft, but stiff in its form. I kiss her, wrapping my arms around her and negating the arm holes. She pulls her arms in. It's thick and warm, hot with our two naked bodies rubbing together. I change my mind and find the armholes, standing on the bed on all fours with Maggie hammocked in the hoodie. I sway swinging her back and forth from side to side while she giggles. She grabs my cock and I push it into her working the hammock effect with me for our pleasure. She reaches for me and wraps her arms around me. I hold her tight and slide off the foot of the bed crawling back onto the bed under the blankets. I roll over pulling her up on top of me in our own little world. We both go for the neck hole at the same time, in need of air and a temperature change. I get there first and find the hood covering my face. She pushes through the humongous neck hole of the size 5X men's hoodie (I'm not exaggerating, I can tell you because I'm facing the tag) and squeezes her arms into the armholes with mine. Suddenly both very snug, we both try to take our arms back out of the sleeves and that doesn't work. I hold the wristbands and she escapes the sleeves. I pull my arms out of the sleeves, but the sleeves join us inside the hoodie. It's like two more arms have joined our sexual escapade. Heads out she reaches around me and grabs my ass with both hands and takes the opportunity to explore my body while she gazes into my eyes.

"I like this," she says. "The sensory experience of exploring your terrain. The vision of your textures and contours can't influence the contact and give me advance notice of what you feel like. It's all new."

I join in on the exploration and get tangled in the sleeves, somehow pulled taut and wound in our bodies and limbs. The more I try to escape the tighter it gets. The drawstring cord in the hood now flops around and smacks me in the face.

She laughs at me, "Are you stuck?"

"Maybe," I half chuckle.

"Let me help," she roots around trying to track the

sleeves. "Shit, the drawstring cord around the bottom is around my thigh. There's no logic here, it's growing from the inside and taking over," she laughs fully aware that a hoodie doesn't have those capabilities.

I worry that this is when I'll find out Maggie has issues with confined spaces or sweat or has to go to the bathroom. But the thought's erased when she bites her lip and gets a devious grin, "Are you up for it?"

"What's it feel like to you?" I push my hard cock at her, poking her body.

She grasps it and strokes it a few times then wriggles up on top of me, and slides down my needy shaft. Her body moving with what range it's allowed. I move with her. The both of us completely in sync. Increasing in pace. Perspiring, our bodies sliding together in the heat and primal need. Friction building. I gaze at her face as her mouth drops open and her eyes glaze, "Oh my god, Drew. I've never been like this before. I'm going to come so fucking hard on your cock. Oh fuck!" She's breathing heavy and so am I. It's all I can do to hold it together as we move together in frantic need.

"You're so fucking good. Oh, my Maggie!"

Our bodies rub against each other. My cock out of control inside her. I can't help myself, I try to get in deeper and she screams out, "Drew! Yes!" As she shatters in ecstasy around me. I shove in deeper until I bottom out, needing as much as I can get, "Oh fuck, Drew!" And I'm rewarded.

"Almost Maggie."

"No, don't stop!"

I do as she says and she whimpers, making the sexiest noises I've ever heard, immediately sending me spiraling over the edge as I release inside her.

I WAKE up when the sunlight hits my window, but this time she's still here with me. Where could she have gone without me when we're stuck in this hoodie?

I kiss her forehead and her eyes open, staring directly at me since she's still on top of me and my cock is still inside her.

We both move and remember the confined space. Smiling she rests her head against my cheek and I couldn't be happier.

"Is this okay?" She asks.

"For as long as you want, my Maggie," my heart beats with hers. "We belong together."

PLAYLIST

"Beautiful People," by The Black Keys
"It's a Long Way to the Top," by AC/DC.
"Lust to Love," by the Go-Go's
"Lonely Boy," Black Keys
"Maggie May," by Rod Stewart
"The Truth," by James Blunt
"A Beautiful Game," by Ed Sheeran
"Dangerous Woman," by Ariana Grande
"I Just Want to Shine," (Acoustic Version) by Fitz and the
Tantrums
"Asleep," by The Smiths
"Here to Forever," (Acoustic Version) by Death Cab for
Cutie
"Play with Fire," by Sam Tinnesz featuring Yacht Money
"Sink," by Noah Kahan
"Always Remember Us This Way," by Lady Gaga

MAGGIE'S PLAYLIST

"You Are The Reason," by Calum Scott
"Missing Piece," by Vance Joy
"Caffeine," by Jack Kays
"Parallel Line," by Keith Urban
"Stick Season," Noah Kahan
"Saturday Sun," by Vance Joy

THE PANTY THIEF

From USA Today Bestselling Author Naomi Springthorp comes a romantic comedy with heat, a cat, and a hottie named Truck.

I've always had my best friend. She's the sister I chose and with me for life. She's also the only roommate I've ever had. Everything was perfect—until she popped out a baby.

I have to move out. I can't sleep in my own bed and I'm waking up everyone in the house when I get home from the club. Nobody wants to hear a crying baby at 3am. Especially when I just left my conquest for the night begging for more.

Crashing at my ex's while I apartment hunt is only a temporary solution.

Now, my bestie is forcing me to have a house warming party —and if I know her at all, she has an ulterior motive.

There's a new hot chick in my building. She's put together and her attitude is off the charts.

I didn't expect her to be a cat lady.

I'm not into her. Women are trouble.

Her scent lingers in the hallway and drives me nuts.

Hitting it in my own building? Not going to happen. It's hard enough to hide being the owner from the tenants. That's extra drama I don't want or need.

The warm sunbeam every afternoon. My favorite treats. They fed me well at the rescue house and the other cats learned I was in charge early on.

The woman with the screaming infant who picked me up was not ideal. However, my new maid and I will get along just fine. She just doesn't know it yet.

Available now from your favorite bookseller...
https://www.books2read.com/pantythief

NAOMI SPRINGTHORP

USA Today Bestselling Author Naomi Springthorp is a born and raised Southern California girl who believes that life has a soundtrack and half of each year should be spent cheering for her favorite baseball team. She loves music and spending time with her feline fur babies.

Naomi writes Baseball Romance, Romantic Comedies, Contemporary Romance, and 90s Throwbacks—all with heat and sometimes a little sweet.

Sign-up for Naomi's newsletter at
www.naomispringthorp.com/sign-up
to get updates on everything she has going on.

facebook.com/naomithewriter

instagram.com/naomispringthorp

amazon.com/author/naomispringthorp

goodreads.com/naomithewriter

bookbub.com/authors/naomi-springthorp

tiktok.com/@naomispringthorp

ALSO BY NAOMI SPRINGTHORP

An All About the Diamond Romance

The Sweet Spot

King of Diamonds

Diamonds in Paradise (a novella)

Star-Crossed in the Outfield

The Closer (a novella)

Falling For Prince (A Short Stop)

Up to Bat

Betting on Love

Just a California Girl

Jacks

Novellas and standalone novels

Muffin Man (a novella)

Finally in Focus (a novella)

Confessions of an Online Junkie

Jonah's Kiss

The Panty Thief

Anthologies & Box Sets

Sacrifice for Love

Storybook Pub

Storybook Pub Christmas Wishes

Storybook Pub 2

Young Crush

Hate to Want You

Tricks, Treats, & Teasers

Caught Under the Mistletoe

Game On

Imperfect Date

Hopelessly Devoted

Ruff Love

ACKNOWLEDGMENTS

Stalking Second has been a long time coming. Life throws curveballs. Thank you to all of you who have supported me, especially my core team who helps me and puts up with me. Special thank you to Samantha for taking some of my tasks away to give me more time to write and being a rockstar PA at events.

As always, thank you to Andie, Irene, Katrina, and Tonya—I wouldn't know what to do without you!

A thankful nod to two of my original Naughties, Jaime and Mary... the details are in the story.

There's more coming...

Love & Baseball Butts,
Naomi